Reginald B. B. Esher

The Yoke of Empire

Sketches of the Queen's Prime Ministers

Reginald B. B. Esher

The Yoke of Empire
Sketches of the Queen's Prime Ministers

ISBN/EAN: 9783337168216

Printed in Europe, USA, Canada, Australia, Japan

Cover: Foto ©Andreas Hilbeck / pixelio.de

More available books at **www.hansebooks.com**

THE

YOKE OF EMPIRE

SKETCHES OF THE QUEEN'S PRIME MINISTERS

BY

REGINALD B. BRETT

ἄρχω πέιθων

London

MACMILLAN AND CO., LIMITED

NEW YORK: THE MACMILLAN COMPANY

1896

THIS VOLUME

IS

DEDICATED

TO THE YOUNGEST OF THE

QUEEN'S

PRIME MINISTERS

PREFACE

In this volume the writer has endeavoured to illustrate a single point—the human relation between a Constitutional Sovereign and her Ministers. Our form of Government may change, and the Victorian legend may become as obsolete as the Elizabethan, but of the imagination of Englishmen both cannot fail to keep fast hold so long as the Empire endures. Meanwhile, to living statesmen, and to those who will follow them, the story indicated in these pages is the primary lesson of that monarchical republic which has been fashioned out of their ancient traditions and their modern necessities by the English people.

CONTENTS

ILLUSTRATIONS

NOTE

THESE chapters, with the exception of the two last, have appeared in the *Nineteenth Century*, and are reprinted with the kind permission of Mr. J. Knowles.

I

THE QUEEN AND HER FIRST PRIME MINISTER

When from the vantage-ground of far-distant centuries men come to look back upon the history of the British Empire, probably no figure will surpass in brilliancy and interest that of Queen Victoria. In order to form a just idea of the strong relief in which the Queen will stand out from her predecessors, it is necessary to imagine Elizabeth known to us by the light of her own utterances and those of her contemporaries; for it is thus that the Queen is revealed to the readers of her journals, her correspondence, and the memoirs of those who have been privileged to observe closely the higher political movement of her reign. The life of the Queen has been laid open to the eyes of all who care to look. It is pure and honest and simple beyond the lives of most women, and harmonises with the fancies upon which idealists have loved to dwell. Emotional, with full play of the higher feelings, tempered by caution and sound reason, the Queen has reigned over half-a-century without making a personal enemy, without creating a political foe. It is a famous record; for the negative virtues are the rarest of all in monarchs. No act of cruelty sullies the rule of Queen Victoria, and, so far as her subjects can judge of her, she has been unjust to none of them. This alone, apart from the lofty moral atmosphere in which she has always moved, is higher praise than any of her ancestors can boast.

It was "in a palace in a garden, meet scene for youth and innocence," as one in later years to be her Minister has said, that she received the news of her accession to a throne overlooking "every sea and nations in every zone." There are but few who would deny that the sequel to her reign has proved worthy of the opening. Seldom has a woman been called upon to play a more difficult part than the young girl, hardly eighteen years old, who in June 1837 stood with bare feet, and in her night-dress, receiving the homage of the Lords who had come to announce to her that she was Queen of England.

The scene has been admirably described. William the Fourth was dead. The Archbishop of Canterbury and Lord Conyngham were despatched to inform the Princess Victoria of the fact. It was a warm night in June. The Princess was sleeping in her mother's room, her custom from childhood, and had to be summoned out of her sleep. The messengers awaited her in the long, unlofty room, separated only by folding-doors from that which was inhabited by the Duchess of Kent and her daughter. The young girl entered alone, in her night-dress, with some loose wrap thrown hastily about her. The moment she was addressed as "Your Majesty" she put out her hand, intimating that the Lords who addressed her were to kiss it, and thereby do homage. Her schooling and her instincts were admirable from the first. Self-possession combined with perfect modesty came naturally to her. A few hours later, at eleven o'clock in the morning, the child-Queen met her Council. In the corridor at Windsor there is a picture which commemorates the event. Never, it has been said by an eye-witness, was anything like the first impression she produced, or the chorus of praise and admiration which was raised about her manner and behaviour, certainly not without justice. Her extreme youth and inexperience, and the ignorance of the world concerning her—for she had lived in complete seclusion—excited interest and curiosity. Asked whether she would enter the room accompanied by the Great Officers of State, she said she would come in alone. Accordingly, when all the Lords of the Privy Council were assembled, the folding-doors were thrown open, and the Queen entered, quite plainly dressed and in mourning, and took her seat for the first time, a young girl among a crowd of men, including all the most famous and powerful of her subjects.

She bowed, and read her speech, handed to her by the Prime Minister, Lord Melbourne, in a clear and firm voice, and then took the oath for the security of the Church of Scotland. Immediately the Privy Councillors were sworn; the royal Dukes of Cumberland and Sussex first by themselves. It was observed that as these two old men, her uncles, knelt before her swearing allegiance, she blushed up to the eyes, as if she felt the contrast between their civil and natural relations. Her manner was very graceful and engaging, and she kissed them both, and, rising from her chair, moved towards the Duke of Sussex, who was too infirm to reach her. She spoke to no one, nor could the smallest difference in her manner be detected, though carefully scrutinised to see whether she drew distinction between Lord Melbourne and the Ministers on the one hand, or the Duke of Wellington and Sir R. Peel on the other. Occasionally, when in doubt what to do, she looked to Lord Melbourne for instruction; but this rarely occurred. No wonder he was charmed; no wonder that Sir R. Peel was amazed at her manner and behaviour, at her apparent deep sense of the situation, at her modesty and her firmness. No wonder that the Duke of Wellington was constrained to admit that if she had been his own daughter he could not have desired to see her perform her part better.

It was not only by her appearance and manner that the Queen made her charm felt. She acted in difficult circumstances with every sort of good taste and good feeling, as well as good sense. To the Queen Dowager her behaviour was perfect. She wrote to her in the kindest terms, begging her to consult only her health and convenience, and to remain at Windsor as long as she pleased. This much any tender-hearted woman might have done; but her thoughtfulness for the feelings of others already was apparent in the smallest and least expected details. When about to go down to visit the Queen Dowager at Windsor, to Lord Melbourne's great surprise she told him that the flag on the Round Tower was flying half-mast high, and that as they would probably elevate it on her arrival, it would be better to send orders beforehand not to do so. He had never thought of the flag, nor did he know anything about it. Attention to details, which some would consider trifles, but which differentiate more than great actions the thoughtful from the thoughtless mind, has from her youth upwards been characteristic of the Queen. Of her good sense and caution ample proof was soon given in her treatment of those who had been about her since childhood. Upon none of them did she exclusively rely. Conroy she dismissed at once, with a pension, from her immediate surroundings. The Baroness Lehzen remained as before her companion. It was noticed that whenever she was asked to decide upon some difficult matter she invariably said she would think it over and reply on the morrow. Men, knowing to what extent she relied upon the advice of Lord Melbourne, imagined that in everything she consulted him. He, however, declared that to many of his questions a similar reply was given.

The Minister was quickly absorbed

by the novel and exciting duty which had fallen to him. No human relation could be more fascinating than that in which he stood to the Queen. Perhaps no man before or since has quite filled the place that Lord Melbourne occupied in the life of a girl who was not his wife or his daughter. For four years he saw the Queen every day. He was formed, as an acute observer noticed, to ingratiate himself with her. The unbounded consideration and respect with which he treated her, his desire to consult her tastes and wishes, the ease of his frank and natural manners, his quaint epigrammatic turn of mind, all helped to charm the girl who was his sovereign, but who also stood to him *in statu pupillari*. The excitement—for it could have been no less to him, a man of the world, with a romantic bias, as well as a keen practical intelligence—of having to guide and direct such a pupil can be well imagined.

He never betrayed his responsibility nor presumed upon his position. It was a piece of rare good fortune which found him Minister at the King's death. With all the immense powers of head and heart which the Queen came later to discover in Sir R. Peel, it is more than doubtful if he could have fulfilled in the summer of 1837 the duties so easily assumed by his rival.

Lord Melbourne's life had been chequered by curious experiences. In the sphere of politics he had found himself on pleasant lines; but in private his lot had been cast with that of a woman versed in all the wearing secrets of romantic passion. To turn from the memory of his wife's wild excesses in thought and language, to the pure-hearted and simple girl whom the Fates had given him as a Queen and a daughter must have touched him to the quick.

Varied as is the business of a Prime Minister, full as his mind must necessarily be of State affairs, Lord Melbourne's absorbing interest became the blossoming of this youthful character under his watchful eye and careful guardianship.

He was no longer young, but he was not old. At the Coronation, after the heroic figure of the Duke of Wellington, it was to Lord Melbourne that the attention of onlookers was mainly directed.

His head was a truly noble one [wrote Leslie, no mean judge]. I think, indeed, he was the finest specimen of manly beauty in the meridian of life I ever saw; not only were his features eminently handsome, but his expression was in the highest degree intellectual. His laugh was frequent, and the most joyous possible, and his voice so deep and musical, that to hear him say the most ordinary things was a pleasure; but his frankness, his freedom from affectation, and his peculiar humour rendered almost everything he said, though it seemed perfectly natural, yet quite original.

Chantrey's bust and the beautiful portraits in the corridor at Windsor—one taken when he was but a boy, the other in middle life—corroborate the view of his contemporaries. His memory was prodigious, and he read voraciously. In classical attainments, including a neat talent for verse, he was up to the high average level of the educated men of his time. In knowledge of history and of politics he was not surpassed by any; and no living Englishman was by age, character, and experience so well qualified for the task which lay under his hand.

That the young Queen should have become attached with almost filial regard to her Minister is not surprising, and that he admirably fulfilled his duty was never questioned by those who knew the truth. Sir R. Peel, his chief political opponent, admitted that the Queen could not do better than take his advice and abide by his counsel; and the Duke of Wellington, then Leader of the Opposition to him in the House of Lords, declared publicly that Lord Melbourne had rendered the greatest possible service by making the Queen acquainted with the mode and policy of government, initiating her into the laws and spirit of the Constitution, and teaching her to preside over the destinies of the country.

The initiation of the Queen into the spirit of the Constitution even Lord Melbourne's political foes felt could not be in better hands; and although the *Times*, then a party journal, declared the all but infant and helpless Queen to be delivered up into the hands of the Whig Minister, and evidently anticipated the worst results from it, these prognostications were happily falsified. Her uncle, the King of the Belgians, and his curious mentor, the physician Stockmar, from the first endeavoured to instil into the Queen's mind her responsibilities as a constitutional sovereign, and the supreme importance of holding an impartial balance between the two great political parties. Had Lord Melbourne been a degree less loyal, had he been an office-seeker, had he possessed an exaggerated belief in his own infallibility, the Queen might not have responded so readily to the wise advice of her relative and of Stockmar. She has allowed the admission to be made on her behalf that between her accession and her marriage, in spite of Lord Melbourne's daily lessons, in reality because of their charm, she had drifted insensibly into political partisanship. Had it been otherwise she would not have been human; but it is to the credit of Lord Melbourne that neither by precept, nor hint, nor suggestion did he encourage his sovereign's bias towards the Whig party. He taught her the duties of queenship in their widest sense.

> No pedagogue could have done this [says one of the most fascinating of biographers]; a professor from one of the universities might have taught her the letters of the Constitution in a course of morning lessons, but he would probably have failed to convey along with it that informing and quickening spirit without which the letter profiteth nothing, or leads to mischief.

He was, as he has been called, a Regius Professor, but with no professional disqualifications; and if to political Crokers, spell the word as you will, his influence seemed dangerous, the Tory leaders recognised the indispensable nature of his task, and acquiesced in his performance of it. He was a Whig, no doubt, says his biographer, but at any rate he was an honest-hearted Englishman, in no merely conventional sense a gentleman, on whose perfect honour no one hesitated to place reliance. He lived at Windsor Castle, and had constant access to the Queen. In the morning he carried and explained to her letters and despatches. After luncheon he rode with her, taking his place next to her. Or he rode by her side when she drove, with the Duchess of Kent, in a low carriage drawn by four white ponies, attended by grooms in scarlet, and a number of gentlemen riding in attendance. Or perhaps it was a review of troops in the park, when her Minister would stand and watch his charge as she rode between the lines, in the Windsor uniform riding-habit, with the blue ribbon of the Garter, and a smart *schako* trimmed with gold lace, returning the salutes of her troops by raising her hand to her cap in true military fashion. "The most fascinating thing ever seen," veteran officers would declare; and can there be any doubt that Lord Melbourne agreed with them in his hearty way? Or he would be still prouder of her when, after bidding farewell to departing relatives, and about to leave the ship, the captain and officers betrayed their anxiety to assist her down the tall side of the vessel, she looked up with the greatest spirit, and said quite loud in her silvery voice, "No help, thank you; I am used to this," and descended, as an eye-witness noticed, "like an old boatswain." It is not, perhaps, astonishing that Lord Melbourne should have joined in the enthusiastic cheers of her sailors. Or he accompanied her on those Sunday afternoons, from four to five, when the band played upon the incomparable terrace at Windsor; and there are those who still remember the crowds of people, thick-set rows of men, women, and Eton boys, pressing round the child-Queen as she walked, her courtiers hardly able to cleave a passage through them, and Lord Melbourne walking half a pace behind her, on her right, stooping a little so as to be quite within earshot; a fascinating sight; the homage of a protector.

Visitors at Windsor were struck with the Minister's manner to the Queen. The mixture of parental anxiety and respectful deference was naturally responded to by her, and she gave him her entire confidence. Greville remarked that he had no doubt Melbourne was passionately fond of her, as he might be of a daughter if he had one, and the more so because he was a man with a great capacity for loving without having anything in the world to love. As they are the impressions of an eye-witness, and a man of discrimination, it is worth while to quote Greville's *Journal* of the 15th December 1838:—

Went on Wednesday to a Council at Windsor, and after the Council was invited to stay that night; rode with the Queen, and after riding, Melbourne came to me and said her Majesty wished me to stay the next day also. This was very gracious and very considerate, because it was done for the express purpose of showing that she was not displeased at my not staying when asked on a former occasion, and as she can have no object whatever in being civil to me, it was a proof of her good nature and thoughtfulness about other people's little vanities, even those of the most insignificant. Accordingly I remained till Friday morning, when I went with the rest of her suite to see the hounds throw off, which she herself saw for the first time. The Court is certainly not gay, but it is perhaps impossible that any Court should be gay where there is no social equality; where some ceremony and a continual air of deference and respect must be observed, there can be no ease, and without ease there can be no real pleasure. The Queen is natural, good-humoured, and cheerful, but still she is Queen, and by her must the social habits and the tone of conversation be regulated, and for this she is too young and inexperienced. She sits at a large round table, her guests around it, and Melbourne always in a chair beside her, where two mortal hours are consumed in such conversation as can be found, which appears to be, and really is, very uphill work. This, however, is the only bad part of the whole; the rest of the day is passed without the slightest constraint, trouble, or annoyance to anybody; each person is at liberty to employ himself or herself as best pleases them, though very little is done in common, and in this respect Windsor is totally unlike any other place. There is none of the sociability which makes the agreeableness of an English country house; there is no room in which the guests assemble, sit, lounge, and talk as they please and when they please; there is a billiard-table, but in such a remote corner of the Castle that it might as well be in the town of Windsor; and there is a library well stocked with books, but hardly accessible, imperfectly warmed, and only tenanted by the librarian: it is a mere library, too, unfurnished, and offering none of the comforts and luxuries of a habitable room. There are two breakfast-rooms, one for the ladies and the guests, and the other for the equerries; but when the meal is over everybody disperses, and nothing but another meal reunites the company, so that, in fact, there is no society whatever, little trouble, little etiquette, but very little resource or amusement.

The life which the Queen leads is this: she gets up soon after eight o'clock, breakfasts in her own room, and is employed the whole morning in transacting business; she reads all the despatches and has every matter of interest and importance in every department laid before her. At eleven or twelve Melbourne comes to her and stays an hour, more or less, according to the business he may have to transact. At two she rides with a large suite (and she likes to have it numerous); Melbourne always rides on her left hand, and the equerry-in-waiting generally on her right; she rides for two hours along the road, and the greater part of the time at a full gallop; after riding she amuses herself for the rest of the afternoon with music and singing, playing, romping with children, if there are any in the Castle (and she is so fond of them that she generally contrives to have some there), or in any other way she fancies. The hour of dinner is nominally half-past seven o'clock, soon after which time the guests assemble, but she seldom appears till near eight. The lord-in-waiting comes into the drawing-room and instructs each gentleman which lady he is to take to dinner. When the guests are all assembled the Queen comes in, preceded by the gentlemen of her household, and followed by the Duchess of Kent and all her ladies; she speaks to each lady, bows to the men, and goes immediately into the dining-room. She generally takes the arm of the man of the highest rank, but on this occasion she went with Mr. Stephenson, the American Minister (though he has no rank), which was very wisely done. Melbourne invariably sits on her left, no matter who may be there; she remains at table the usual time, but does not suffer the men to sit long after her, and we were summoned to coffee in less than a quarter of an hour. In the drawing-room she never sits down till the men make their appearance. Coffee is served to them in the adjoining room, and then they go into the drawing-room, when she goes round and says a few words to each, of the most trivial nature, all, however, very civil and cordial in manner and expression. When this little ceremony is over, the Duchess of Kent's whist table is arranged, and then the round table is marshalled, Melbourne invariably sitting on the left hand of the Queen, and remaining there without moving till the evening is at an end. At about half-past eleven she goes to bed, or whenever the Duchess has played her usual number of rubbers, and the band have performed all the pieces on their list for the night. This is the whole history of her day: she orders and regulates every detail herself, she knows where everybody is lodged in the

Castle, settles about the riding or driving, and enters into every particular with minute attention. But while she personally gives her orders to her various attendants, and does everything that is civil to all the inmates of the Castle, she really has nothing to do with anybody but Melbourne, and with him she passes (if not in *tête-à-tête*, yet in intimate communication) more hours than any two people, in any relation of life, perhaps ever do pass together besides. He is at her side for at least six hours every day—an hour in the morning, two on horseback, one at dinner, and two in the evening. This monopoly is certainly not judicious; it is not altogether consistent with social usage, and it leads to an infraction of those rules of etiquette which it is better to observe with regularity at Court. But it is more peculiarly inexpedient with reference to her own future enjoyment, for if Melbourne should be compelled to resign, her privations will be the more bitter on account of the exclusiveness of her intimacy with him. Accordingly, her terror when any danger menaces the Government, her nervous apprehension at any appearance of change, affect her health, and upon one occasion during the last session she actually fretted herself into an illness at the notion of their going out. It must be owned that her feelings are not unnatural, any more than those which Melbourne entertains towards her. His manner to her is perfect, always respectful, and never presuming upon the extraordinary distinction he enjoys; hers to him is simple and natural, indicative of the confidence she reposes in him, and of her lively taste for his society, but not marked by any unbecoming familiarity. Interesting as his position is, and flattered, gratified, and touched as he must be by the confiding devotion with which she places herself in his hands, it is still marvellous that he should be able to overcome the force of habit so completely as to endure the life he leads. Month after month he remains at the Castle, submitting to this daily routine; of all men he appeared to be the last to be broken in to the trammels of a Court, and never was such a revolution seen in anybody's occupations and habits. Instead of indolently sprawling in all the attitudes of luxurious ease, he is always sitting bolt upright; his free and easy language, interlarded with "damns," is carefully guarded and regulated with the strictest propriety, and he has exchanged the good talk of Holland House for the trivial, laboured, and wearisome inanities of the Royal circle.

Greville noticed that the Queen never ceased to be Queen, and that all her naïveté, kindness, and good-nature were combined with the propriety and dignity demanded by her lofty station.

Lord Melbourne had been in public life for many years, and since 1835 he had been Prime Minister; but as leader of the Whig party, and as a statesman, although he had exhibited skill, and occasionally power, he had never shown himself to be indispensable, or to be filling an office that could not have been equally well filled by half-a-dozen of his contemporaries. Now, however, all was changed. The importance of his work, as is commonly the case, was at the time not fully appreciated. Doubtless far more interest was felt in the controversial questions of domestic politics which then divided parties; and the respective attitudes of Lord Durham and Lord Brougham were thought to have far deeper influence on public affairs than the relation of the Queen to her Minister.

In reality, however, the inevitable Irish question, troubles in Egypt, missions to Afghanistan, Persian wars, all important in their way, sink into insignificance beside the great political event which was exclusively controlled by Lord Melbourne when he undertook to form the political character of the Queen.

It is difficult to over-estimate the value to England and to the Empire of the four years of teaching which the Queen received at Lord Melbourne's hands.

It is possible to exaggerate the effect produced by such admirable letters as those of the King of the Belgians, and the sound dogmatising of Baron Stockmar; but Lord Melbourne's daily culture of the Queen's mind, his careful pruning away of extraneous growths harmful in a constitutional sovereign, his respectful explanation of her duties, cannot have failed to have rendered her more fit to receive and profit by the closer friend and guide who was to follow, and whose teaching was in a great degree a variation upon the text of the Whig Minister.

Speculation staggers at the prospect of what might have occurred if Queen Victoria had exhibited the obstinacy of her grandfather, or the partisanship of Queen Anne, or the unconscientious neglect of duty so conspicuous in George the Fourth. Those first four years of her reign were crucial in their importance to the formation of her character as a sovereign and a woman. From their novelty and excitement they must have left the young girl in a mental state only too ready to receive lifelong impressions of good or evil. The Queen has said that they were years full of peril for her, and has expressed her gratitude that none of her children have had to run the risk she believes herself to have incurred. It was England's good fortune as well as the Queen's that at such a moment Lord Melbourne's guiding hand was held out to her.

In spite of all that he could do to inure her to the idea, it soon became clear that the Queen viewed with dismay a change of Ministers which would deprive her of his advice and companionship ; her feelings, when strongly stirred, have always been but partially under control ; and when the crisis of his ministerial fate arrived in May 1839, Lord Melbourne's earnest endeavour to smooth the way for Sir Robert Peel was not altogether successful.

The "Bedchamber Question" seems

by the light of subsequent years to have admitted of only one proper solution; and that Lord Melbourne showed want of foresight in not preparing the Queen's mind for the inevitable change in the *personnel* of her Court, and want of resolution in advising her to yield to Sir Robert Peel's strong representations, has never in recent years been denied. The temptation was strong to support her in her maidenly desire not to part with the Duchess of Sutherland and other ladies who had been around her since her accession; while party tacticians derived hopeful satisfaction from the capital which they hoped to make of Ministerial devotion to the person of the youthful sovereign, and of self-immolation upon the altar of her natural feelings. As is obvious from his subsequent life, Lord Melbourne, when the moment of parting came, was singularly loth to leave his pupil while any chance remained which enabled him to continue to live the engrossing life of the past two years.

It came to pass, however, that the Princess of nineteen was strong enough to overturn a great Ministerial combination ; that in doing so she was supported by the Whig party ; that the phrase, "I have stood by you : you must now stand by me," in the mouth of a sovereign, successfully appealed to one of the house of Russell ; that the charming petulance of the cry, "They wish to treat me like a girl, but I will show them I am Queen of England," went unchallenged at a Whig Cabinet ; and that the doctrine that the *principle* was not maintainable, but that they were bound *as gentlemen* to support the Queen, actually decided a Whig Government to continue to enjoy for two years a further term of office. Such is the force of the human element in great affairs, to the confusion of doctrinaires, and of unfortunate devotees of science.

Possibly some kind divinity interposed to assist the Queen at this moment, pregnant as it was with a change vital to her reign, as well as to her personal happiness ; for in a few short months it was to Lord Melbourne, a real friend of comparative long standing, rather than to a stranger, however kindly disposed, that she came to announce her intention of asking Prince Albert of Saxe-Coburg to become her consort; and it was not from formal lips, but from the heart of her Minister and friend, that the words of approval and congratulation flowed. No one else could have said to her in homely language, "You will be very much more comfortable, for a woman cannot stand alone for any time, in whatever position she may be"; and no one during the trying months that followed, in which the joys of a love-match were curiously blended with painful discussions in Parliament, and hateful but necessary public arrangements, could have filled adequately Lord Melbourne's place in the eyes of the fatherless girl who stood alone, without a male friend or protector of any kind. It is not surprising that at the Council, when she announced her approaching marriage, her nervousness should have permitted her to notice only the kindly face of her Prime Minister, and still less wonderful is it that in that momentary glance she should have seen that his eyes were full of tears. The prevision of work well-nigh accomplished must have rushed upon him with full and saddening force, and the feeling of pleasure in the Queen's happiness must have been shot with sorrow at the thought of the fascinating tutelage which was about to end.

During the eighteen months that followed the 10th of February 1840, when the Queen was married, to the 31st of August 1841, when Sir Robert Peel was sent for by the Queen, her Minister was engaged in the task of providing himself with a successor. For it was only in a limited sense that Peel took his predecessor's place, and the real successor to Lord Melbourne, in influence, in authority, and in guidance, was Prince Albert, a mere boy in years, but who had been so carefully trained, and was happily endowed with such singular powers of self-control in one so young, that he from the first seemed to experience no difficulty in taking Lord Melbourne's place at the side of the Queen. It was as though a guardian had relinquished his trust; and with the fall of the Melbourne Government the reign of the Queen may be said to have come of age.

For some time the end of the Administration was seen to be approaching, and abnormal perception in reading political signs was not required to forecast the result of an appeal to the country whenever it should take place; but Lord Melbourne's fall, though generally welcomed, carried with it an unusual degree of personal pain to the Sovereign and her Minister. Notwithstanding his regret, Lord Melbourne took leave of the Queen with his usual cheerful smile, although the pathos of parting from something more cherished than political power rings in the almost familiar words of farewell which she herself has recorded. He pretended that his principal sorrow was for her, but in reality his was the heavier burden. "For four years I have seen you every day; but it is so different now to what it would have been in 1839." It was different, no doubt, and it was Lord Melbourne above all who was about to feel the quality of the difference.

During the leave-taking the Queen admits that she was much affected, and that the separation from her old friend was a trying time for her, when all the consolation which her husband could give her was required. This was freely bestowed, and the exigencies of her great position speedily reinvolved her in affairs of State, clouding regrets in the dust of strenuous and constant duty.

To Lord Melbourne, however, the end of life had come. He was sixty-three, still young as the days of statesmen are now counted, but his work was done and his mission fulfilled. He had placed the sceptre and globe in the hands of the youthful Sovereign, and there was no further need for him in the world.

The truth seemed to strike him with overwhelming force, and although he tried to simulate a continued interest in public affairs, and to persuade himself that he was yet in full career, the melancholy of hopelessness gradually enveloped him, and threw into deep shadow the remaining years of his life. To resume old habits, to turn to the classics, to books, to old friends anxious to welcome him, or to new ones eager for his society, seemed alike impossible. The reaction was too great, and the difference between what was and what had been too profound.

Into a solitary and loveless life the most thrilling human element had been accidentally introduced, and, like Silas Marner, who, expectant of mere gold coin, suddenly found the golden head of a child, so Lord Melbourne, in the lottery of political life, obtained not only the first place, but a prize from which the wifeless and childless man could not find himself bereft without complete loss of mental balance. It is painful to lift the veil from those last sad years, when at Brocket, the home of his youth, the ex-Minister slowly sank into the grave.

Hearts break oftener than is generally supposed, and they are cleft upon curious and unnoticed angles. Many attempts were made, by the Queen herself and others, to rouse the drooping spirit of one whose name is associated with a nature almost reckless in its *insouciance* and gaiety; but they were fruitless. When the end finally came, no one grieved more deeply than the Lady whose debt to him was so heavy, and was so fully recognised. It was some consolation to feel that during the last "melancholy years of his life" his pupil and her husband had been often the "chief means of giving him" fitful gleams of pleasure; and no one can doubt the sincerity of the passage in the Queen's Journal which records how "truly and sincerely" she deplored "the loss of one who was a most kind and disinterested friend of mine, and most sincerely attached to me"—one who was, "for the first two years and a half of my reign, almost the only friend I had."

It may be the tendency of modern times to look less upon individual character than upon vast masses of nameless men as the determining factor in great public affairs, so that hereafter Englishmen may come to view the history of their race much as some of us gaze upon the stars, with an indefinite and confused sense of glory, the riddle of which we cannot read; but it is impossible that those who look back to the reign of Queen Victoria should not pause for a moment, held in thrall by the moving figure of the girl-Queen, stepping as it were from innocent sleep, with bare feet and dazzled eyes, upon the slippery steps of her throne, supported by the tender and respectful hand of the first of her long series of Prime Ministers.

II

THE QUEEN AND HER SECOND PRIME MINISTER

When Lord Melbourne became the Queen's Prime Minister on her accession in 1837, she was a young girl only a few days over eighteen years of age. When Lord Melbourne was succeeded by Sir Robert Peel in 1841, the Queen was still a girl in years, but she was twenty-two and married. Under the gentle auspices of Lord Melbourne the girl-Princess had become a woman and a queen. Sir Robert Peel's task was a very different one. By the Queen's side he found a prince three months younger than the Sovereign, a foreigner by birth, full of keen intellectual interests, of singularly strong and masterful character, absorbed by honourable ambition to

utilise powers he was conscious of possessing, and yet, owing to the jealous regard of English statesmen in former times, precluded by constitutional usage from taking his place on the throne beside his wife. The Queen had been anxious to make her husband King-Consort, and indeed had strained every nerve to bring it about; but Lord Melbourne had turned a deaf ear to hints and suggestions, and it was only when he met her plain request by the rough though not unfriendly remark, "For God's sake let's hear no more of it, ma'am; if you once get the English people into the habit of making kings, you may get them into the habit of unmaking them," that the subject was dropped.

Sir Robert Peel, when he took office in 1841, found the Queen's husband her friend and secretary, but when he quitted office in 1847 he left Prince Albert in fact, though not in name, coequal Sovereign and King-Consort. Up to the time of the birth of the Princess Royal the Queen alone possessed pass-keys of all the official boxes which were sent by the Ministers to the Palace. That event saw the first advance in the political position of the Prince, for he was then put in possession of duplicate keys and established as private secretary to the Queen; but when, four years afterwards, Lord John Russell went to Windsor at a crisis in the destinies of Sir Robert Peel's Government, he could not fail to notice the great change that had taken place.

Formerly, as he knew, the Queen received her Ministers alone; they communicated with her only, although they were aware that everything was known to Prince Albert; but now the Queen and the Prince together received Lord Lansdowne and Lord John Russell, and both of them, where the first person singular had been used, now employed the first person plural.

If Lord Melbourne's instinct was adverse to an official recognition of the Prince as king, others, including Stockmar, were equally opposed to the idea, and though the Queen's tenacity induced her to reopen the question with Sir Robert Peel, the Prince's sound judgment prompted him to see that the point was not pressed. To Peel, however, the Prince owed, as the Queen herself has affirmed, his introduction into public life. It was natural that a nature so intense, so full of romantic zeal to act rightly, and withal so self-commanding as that of Prince Albert, should appeal to the new Prime Minister. The difficulty lay at first in the seeds of prejudice which had been sown in the mind of the Queen by the action of Peel himself when leader of the Opposition to Lord Melbourne's Government. Two years before her marriage the Queen had occasion to meet Sir Robert Peel under circumstances which had galled and pained her, and if her behaviour to him personally had been perfectly kind, the dislike with which she regarded him as a successor to Lord Melbourne had become obvious to those about the Court. The resignation of her Ministers in May of that year had been altogether unexpected by her, and Lord John Russell has related that, during her interview with him, the young Sovereign was dissolved in tears ;

that afterwards she remained secluded for a whole day, refusing to dine as usual with her courtiers, and invisible to them all. Upon Lord Melbourne's advice, however, she sent for the Duke of Wellington, and before seeing him she had regained her composure. The Duke of Wellington, Tory as he was, adopted a position which in these days is supposed to be the special privilege of Radical politicians; and in refusing to be Prime Minister he relied mainly on a view, now a mere pious opinion, that that post should always be held by a member of the House of Commons. When he urged the Queen to send for Peel, whatever her reluctance may have prompted, she consented at once, and upon the Duke suggesting that it would be more in accordance with usage that she should herself write to the man who was about to be her Minister, she did so without comment, merely requesting the Duke to mention to him that he would receive a communication asking him to repair to the Palace. Peel has recorded that when he arrived in full dress, according to custom, somewhat doubtful of his reception, he was received extremely well, and left the Queen perfectly satisfied, having accepted the responsibility of attempting to form a Government.

In order to appreciate the impression made upon the Queen by Peel, it is necessary to picture him as he then was in the prime of life; a man of great vigour, tall and manly, in his fiftieth year only, but with almost thirty years of parliamentary and official life marked on his face. His political career commenced when he was a lad of twenty-two. Three years later he was Chief Secretary for Ireland, and he had been ever since that time one of the most conspicuous figures in the House of Commons. Now he was fifty, and on the eve of becoming, with the exception of the Duke of Wellington, the most prominent Englishman of his day. In some respects he was a new type, and belonged to a new order of statesmen. Sprung from a mercantile stock, he possessed the defects and virtues which are inherent in the provincial middle class. He was essentially, as has been well said of constitutional statesmen, a man of common opinions though of uncommon abilities; and while in thought and ideas other men laboured, he entered into their labours. If he was devoid of all originality of mind, he was rich, decorous, hard-working, and had devoted himself regularly to the task of politics. In appearance when young, when his hair was brown and curly, he struck Mr. Disraeli as the possessor of a very radiant expression of countenance; he appeared to Carlyle later in life as a man

> finely made, of strong, not heavy, rather of elegant stature; stands straight, head slightly thrown back, and eyelids modestly drooping; every way mild and gentle, yet with less of that fixed smile than portraits give him. . . . Clear, strong blue eyes, which kindle on occasion, voice extremely good, low toned, something of cooing in it, rustic, affectionate, honest, mildly persuasive; . . . reserved, seemingly, by nature; obtrudes nothing of diplomatic reserve; on the contrary, a vein of mild fun in him; real sensibility to the ludicrous.

Another physical attribute noticed by the shrewd old Scot is curious. On some occasion, when Peel was showing off his gallery of pictures at Bath House, and in so doing spread his hand over that of Dr. Johnson in Reynolds's well-known portrait, to illustrate some anecdote, Carlyle observed that it was "as fine a man's hand as I remember to have seen, strong, delicate, and scrupulously clean."

It may be thought that the qualities which Carlyle found to his taste were not necessarily appreciable by a young girl. Greville, whose point of view was somewhat different from that of the Scottish poet, was present at the first dinner which the Queen gave to her Minister. He observed that while she talked to her new much as she used to do to her old Ministers, and made no difference in her manner to them, Peel when spoken to could not help putting himself into his "accustomed attitude of a dancing-master giving lessons"; and he charitably suggests that she would have liked him better if he could have kept his legs still.

In the drawing-room, after dinner, Lord Melbourne's chair had gone, and the Lord-in-Waiting had orders to put the Ministers down to whist, while the Queen sat at her round table, with Lord Melbourne no more, but flanked by two ladies, whom Greville evidently thought scarcely capable of sustaining the burden of companionship for a whole evening. Bishop Wilberforce said of Peel that in his family he was reserved and shy : that he had the air of a man conscious of great powers and slight awkwardnesses, and this failure in manner was not limited to his domestic circle, for the Queen told Lord Melbourne that she found Peel so shy that it made her shy, and rendered intercourse difficult and embarrassing. Melbourne anticipated that this would wear off, and wear off it did, as the acquaintance between Peel and Prince Albert, and consequently between Peel and the Queen, ripened into regard and friendship.

The new Minister believed, he had been frequently told, that the Queen looked upon him with mistrust and dislike ; and this hostility was known to have originated in the disputes called by the slang name of the "Bedchamber

Plot," when Peel's manner, even though his contention may have been sound, was said to have been peremptory and harsh. Lord Grey's considerable experience of Court politics drove him to the conclusion that, although Peel was without Court favour, and although his manners and character were not best calculated to obtain it in the eyes of a young Queen of twenty-two, yet if he were prudent and conciliatory, he had no doubt of his successfully making his position secure and comfortable. If Lord Grey had no doubts, Peel had many, and he had been given to understand that the Queen's dislike of him would lead her to "trip up his heels whenever she could."

Lord Melbourne had done his best to assure Peel that these suspicions were ill founded, and so anxious was he to bring about a good understanding between the Sovereign and the man he felt sure would some day inevitably be her Minister, that it showed itself in queer ways and at unexpected moments. At a Court ball more than a year before he quitted office, he noticed that Peel stood proudly aloof, and going up to him he whispered with great earnestness, "For God's sake, go and speak to the Queen." Peel made no move, but it was said at the time that both entreaty and refusal were eminently characteristic of the two men.

When, however, it became necessary for Peel to "speak to the Queen," no one could have behaved with finer tact. Almost the first declaration he made to her was to the effect that if any other ministerial arrangement had been possible, or if any other individual could have been substituted for him, as far as his own personal inclinations were concerned, he should have been most ready to give way. He took great care to explain everything to her, both his proposals and his reasons for them. He adopted Lord Melbourne's advice not to suffer any appointment he was about to make to be talked of publicly, until he had first communicated with her. "The Queen," said Lord Melbourne, "is not conceited; she is aware there are many things she cannot understand, and she likes to have them explained to her elementarily, not at length and in detail, but shortly and clearly; neither does she like long audiences, and I never stayed with her a long time." It would have been well if all her Ministers had borne this advice in mind; for who can doubt that the Queen has suffered much at the hands of prolix political enthusiasts, who have treated her as though she were not a woman but a man, and not a sovereign but a public meeting?

Almost immediately after his first audiences, Peel announced himself to be not only satisfied, but charmed, and declared that the Queen's behaviour to him had been perfect. He had assured her that his first and greatest care should be to consult her happiness and comfort, and that he would take upon himself the responsibility of putting an extinguisher on the personal claim of any one to be near her who should be disagreeable to her or to whom she was disinclined; and the Queen never found her Minister swerving from this duty. Indeed, he may have carried his desire to be agreeable rather further than was consistent with due regard for the claims of his political friends, and certainly much further than they would be carried by any Minister in these days. To some extent this was forced upon him by the difficulty of following Lord Melbourne in office. He could not afford to be as unceremonious as his predecessor, and he was obliged to be more facile. When he refused to dine with the Lord Mayor in the first November of his Premiership, on the ground that he was commanded to the Palace, it was observed that Lord Melbourne under similar circumstances would have gone to the Guildhall. Peel did not think he could afford to excuse himself to the Queen; and men marvelled at the frequency with which his visits to the Palace were repeated.

At her first Council with her new Ministers, an occasion of severe trial, the Queen conducted herself with a dignity and self-control that excited in them the greatest admiration. It was noticed that she looked very much flushed, and her heart and eyes were evidently brimful of tears, but she was perfectly composed, and throughout the whole of the proceedings—the farewells of her old Ministers, the friends who had stood about her at her accession, the surrender of their Seals or Wands of Office, and the transference of these to new men, most of whom were unknown to her—she preserved her self-possession, composure, and dignity. In so young a woman it was thought a great effort of self-control, upon an occasion which might well have elicited uncontrollable emotions. The dejection which Peel had noticed during his first interview, when she expressed deep regret at parting with her Ministers, had almost disappeared, thanks to the dignified kindness with which he had assured her of his desire to serve her, and the good taste of his declaration that he had never presumed to anticipate being sent for, and had had no communication with anybody, and was quite unprepared with any suggestions. This was a *coup de maître*, and from that moment the Queen's revulsion of feeling in favour of her Minister may be presumed to have commenced. Many attitudes that towards a monarch might by some be considered as subservient, when the monarch is a woman become merely the high-bred homage due from the stronger to the frailer sex. Before Peel had been many months in office he had vanquished the dislike of the Queen, and had laid the foundation of a regard on her side that never was shaken.

If to a large extent this was due to the pains which he took to ingratiate himself with her, it was mainly owing to the circumstance that in Prince Albert he found a ready sympathiser and a congenial friend. The admiration of these two remarkable men was mutual. Sir Robert Peel had been introduced to Prince Albert by Lord Melbourne some months before the latter retired from office, but this acquaintanceship had not been followed up by any closer intercourse; so that, when the new Minister found himself necessarily thrown with the Prince, he was still embarrassed by the feeling that the Prince might bear malice for the part which he had taken during the debates on the Marriage Settlement, the effect of which had been seriously to curtail the income proposed by Lord Melbourne. In the Prince's demeanour not a shade of soreness could be traced, and Peel was touched. To Lord Kingsdown he said that he had found Prince Albert one of the most extraordinary young men he had ever met; and although so little was then known of the Prince that the expression may have appeared exaggerated, it seems trite enough by the light of fuller knowledge.

> His aptitude for business was wonderful; the dullest and most intricate matters did not escape or weary his attention; his judgment was very good; his readiness to listen to any suggestion, though against his own opinions, was constant;—

and these were all qualities which were bound to excite the attention and attract the sympathies of Peel. There was, it is true, a closer bond which united the two men, the unswerving fortitude with which they both braved misrepresentation.

> Every imaginable calumny is heaped upon us, especially upon me; and although a pure nature, conscious of its own high purposes, is, and ought to be, lifted above attacks; still, it is painful to be misrepresented by people of whom one believed better things.

These words, written by Prince Albert at a time when his popularity was far from great, mere boy as he was, with the English people, might well with equal truth have been written by Peel two years afterwards, when the storm of obloquy broke over him. It was natural that minds, both proud, both reserved, both anxious always to do right, both misunderstood, should have drawn closely together. Before he had been two years her Minister, the Queen wrote to Peel that he was "undoubtedly a great statesman, a man who thinks but little of party, and never of himself"; and the Prince was already full of admiration at the resolve shown by the Minister to adopt his own line, and not to be turned aside from what he believed to be desirable by the fear of making political enemies or of losing support. After his death Peel's character was summed up by the Prince in words which carried the warm approval of the Queen :—

The constitution of Sir Robert Peel's mind was peculiarly that of a statesman, and of an English statesman : he was Liberal from feeling, but Conservative upon principle. While his impulses drove him to foster progress, his sagacious mind and great experience showed him how easily the whole machinery of a state and of society is deranged; and how important, but how difficult also, it is to direct its further development in accordance with its fundamental principles, like organic growth in nature. It was peculiar to him that in great things, as in small, all the difficulties and objections occurred to him; first he would anxiously consider them, pause, and warn against rash resolutions; but having convinced himself, after a long and careful investigation, that a step was not only right to be taken, but of the practical mode also of safely taking it, it became a necessity and a duty to him to take it; all his caution and apparent timidity changed into courage and power of action, and at the same time readiness cheerfully to make any personal sacrifice which its execution might demand.

If the Prince owed to Sir Robert Peel his initiation into public life, he also acquired from him much knowledge of the people over whom, in conjunction with the Queen, he was about to rule. There was something singularly attractive in the intimacy of the two men so different in age and education and training. Peel acted as moderator of the youthful enthusiasms of the Prince for reform, although he gave him invaluable assistance in the changes which the Prince introduced into the customs of the English Court.

Many abuses were, thanks to the Prince, swept away; and thanks to Peel this was done without a great outcry from the manifold interests involved. Peel was full of hearty praise of the wise and judicious economy founded upon good management and order in the Queen's household, under the eye of Prince Albert. To this he bore a strong testimony in the House of Commons; and the simple domestic tastes of the Queen and her husband, no less than their profound delight in natural beauty, suggested to Peel the desirability of the Isle of Wight as a place of retreat for them. Osborne was brought to the notice of the Queen by him, as a spot where privacy and repose could be ensured, and which, at the same time, was sufficiently near to the seat of Government to afford no great inconvenience to her Ministers.

It was entirely through Sir Robert Peel [the Queen once wrote], who knew how much we wished for a private property, and his extreme kindness, that we heard of and all about Osborne. When we showed him all we had done in 1849, he spoke, with evident pleasure, of his having been the means of our getting it.

The Queen had had an opportunity of estimating the domestic taste of her Minister, for within two years of his taking office she had visited his home at Drayton. The visit gave great pleasure to Peel, although it cost him many an ill-natured jest; his entertainments were cruelly criticised, and the fact that the proud and reserved Minister had actually condescended to dance before the Queen supplied the wits of the press with subject for endless mockery. Raleigh's cloak for the feet of Elizabeth was said to be dry commonplace compared with the gallantry of Sir Robert, who offered himself up as a dancer for her Majesty's diversion. It was as if the Archbishop of Canterbury had performed on a tight-rope. All this cheap wit, and the gibes of the *Morning Chronicle*, although the pride of Peel may have chafed under them, only served to strengthen the mutual regard of the Queen and her Minister; for Peel grew rapidly in the good graces of the Sovereign. During her journey to Scotland, accompanied by Sir Robert Peel and Lord Aberdeen, the Prime Minister constantly travelled and drove with the Queen, leaving his own carriage to be occupied by his private secretary, Mr. Drummond; and it was to this special mark of favour that he owed his life, since the madman who shortly afterwards shot the unfortunate Drummond did so under the delusion that the man he had so often seen driving in Peel's carriage must be the Minister himself. When the Queen was abroad on a visit to the King of the French, Peel's "cheering letters" were anxiously awaited, and especially was this the case owing to the fear then entertained that her Minister might sink under the weight of unpopularity which was beginning to gather round him. A short while before, when the Maynooth Bill had sapped the foundations of his power, the Queen, to mark her sense of the importance of the measure and her confidence in Peel, had offered him the Garter. It was refused on grounds characteristic of him : that his heart was not set on titles of honour or social distinctions ; that he sprang from the people and was essentially of the people ; that in his case such honour would be misapplied ; that the only distinction he coveted at her hands was that the Queen should say to him, "You have been a faithful servant, and have done your duty to your country and to myself."

That this opinion was entertained by his royal mistress he already well knew, for she had sent to him a letter written by King Leopold in warm terms which she had more than endorsed :—

> Peel works so hard and has so much to do [the Queen wrote] that he sometimes says he does not know how he is to get through it all. . . . In these days a Minister *does* require some encouragement, for the abuse and difficulties he has to contend with are dreadful.

If such opinions were expressed to and about Sir Robert Peel, his appreciation of them is curious and worth noting :—

Sir R. Peel is scarcely less obliged to your Majesty for your goodness in communicating to him the favourable opinion which King Leopold has been pleased to express of the course of public policy, pursued with the sanction, and frequently under the special direction, of your Majesty, by Sir R. Peel. His Majesty has an intimate knowledge of this country, and is just so far removed from the scene of political contention here as to be able to take a clear and dispassionate view of the motives and acts of public men. Sir R. Peel looks to no other reward, apart from your Majesty's favourable opinion, than that posterity shall hereafter confirm the judgment of King Leopold, that Sir R. Peel was a true and faithful servant of your Majesty, and used the power committed to him for the maintenance of the honour and just prerogatives of the Crown and the advancement of the public welfare. He would, indeed, be utterly unworthy if, after the generous confidence and support which he has invariably received from your Majesty, he could have used power for any other purposes.

If he could write in these terms to the Sovereign, in his *Memoirs* he wrote with even greater warmth :—

I will not say more than that the generous support which I had uniformly received from her Majesty and from the Prince, and all that passed on the occasion of the retirement, made an impression on my heart that can never be effaced. I could not say less than this without doing violence to feelings of grateful and dutiful attachment.

When Peel was forced to resume office preparatory to carrying out his repeal of the Corn Law, his "unbounded loyalty, courage, patriotism, and high-mindedness" were noted by the Queen in her Journal, and she speaks enthusiastically of his "chivalry" to her, and the "excitement and determination" which he exhibited in what he thought so good a cause. "We are *seelenfroh*" (glad in soul), wrote Prince Albert, "at the arrangement under which the Prime Minister remains in office"; and there was no doubt of the sentiments of the Court, although a paper so bitterly hostile to Peel as the *Examiner* recognised the "scrupulous observance of constitutional rules which marked the conduct" of the Queen at that trying time.

The parting between the Queen and her Minister could not, however, be long delayed. When it came, there were poignant regrets on both sides.

Peel may have sighed with relief at escaping from the cares of office, noble as these then were ; but his parting from the Queen cost him some tears.

> Yesterday [the Queen wrote to King Leopold] was a very hard day for me. I had to part with Sir Robert Peel and Lord Aberdeen, who are irreparable losses to us and to the country. They were both so much overcome that it quite upset me, and we have in them two devoted friends. We felt so safe with them. Never during the five years that they were with me did they ever recommend a person or a thing that was not for my or the country's best, and never for the party's advantage only. . . .

Few men who knew Peel as a Minister, and even in his home life, would have readily believed him capable of a display of emotion. His composure and powerful self-command in Parliament were compared to those similar qualities in Mr. Pitt by Lord Stratford, who had seen both of them in turn lead the House of Commons. It is true that a few men, Bishop Wilberforce for one, had noted the tenderness of nature which underlay the cold husk which

Peel turned outward to the world. The Queen had had experience of this on a previous occasion, for in early days of her intercourse with him, after the attempt upon her life by Bean, Sir Robert Peel hurried up from Cambridge to consult with the Prince, and upon the Queen entering the room she was surprised to see the Minister, in public so cold and self-commanding, unable to control his emotion, and burst into tears.

Self-repression was the rule with Peel, and these revelations of the real man were rare. It was once said that his temper was *really* bad, morose, and sullen, but if so these characteristics were never obvious during the months of furious temptation to which he was subjected by his political foes. During the four years that Sir Robert Peel lived after his fall from power there was no cessation of intercourse between him and the Queen. In him the Queen and the Prince found an adviser to whom they could always turn with perfect reliance on his disinterestedness and sincerity. He ceased to be the leader of a party, and for this reason he found himself able to correspond with the Prince "without saying a word of which the most jealous or sensitive successor in the confidence of the Queen could complain."

Although ostracised from political office, no living Englishman at that time stood higher in the opinion of moderate men of both parties. "Everybody," Greville wrote, "asks with anxiety what he says, what he thinks, and what he will do." When for a few hours after his fatal accident he lay dying, the whole nation watched by his bedside; the entrance to his house was besieged by immense crowds, and the sadness upon the faces of his friends as they passed from the door was reflected in the eyes of thousands who had never known him by sight. When he was dead the Queen wrote, "The sorrow and grief at his death are most touching, and the country mourns over him as a father. Every one seems to have lost a personal friend"; and these words were endorsed, as the Queen's words often have been during her reign, by the sentiments of her people. "We have lost," said the Prince, "our truest friend and trustiest counsellor, the throne its most valiant defender, the country its most open-minded and greatest statesman." The character of Sir Robert Peel has often been placed in various lights by those who knew him, who admired and liked him, or who admired and hated him. The Duke of Wellington, in a voice broken with emotion, bore testimony to the love of truth which animated the great commoner under whom he had been willing to serve. Mr. Gladstone, in characteristic words, has laid stress on his qualities of ability, sagacity, indefatigable industry, his sense of public virtue, and his purity of conscience.

The encomiums of friends may be sweet enough to the heart and ear, but they are not those by which a man of disinterested mind would soonest find himself judged worthily. To men like the Duke of Wellington or Mr. Gladstone, who served under him, to the Queen and Prince, whom he served so faithfully, Peel's character would naturally appear exalted by the shadow of death. As his epitaph, it would perhaps be better to let stand the famous passage in which Mr. Disraeli, in his inimitable and epigrammatic style, summed up the character and career of the Minister he had so bitterly opposed. He was not,

> notwithstanding his unrivalled powers of despatching affairs, the greatest Minister this country ever produced, because, twice placed at the helm, and on the second occasion with the Court and Parliament equally devoted to him, he never could maintain himself in power. Nor, notwithstanding his consummate parliamentary tactics, was he the greatest of party leaders, for he contrived to destroy the most compact, powerful, and devoted party that ever followed a statesman. Nor, notwithstanding his great sway in debate, was he the greatest of orators, for in many of the supreme requisites of oratory he was singularly deficient. But what he really was, and what posterity will acknowledge him to have been, is the greatest Member of Parliament that ever lived. Peace to his ashes! His name will be often appealed to in that scene which he loved so well, and never without homage even by his opponents.

If, when those lines were written, they fell under the notice of the Sovereign, she must have read them with mixed feelings of acquiescence in their truth, and of resentment against the hand that had penned them. It must have seemed then to her and the Prince almost a sacrilege to find the memory of the friend and adviser, so recently honoured, treated with qualified though warm approval by the politician who in life had so bitterly traduced him. Yet time has curious revenges; for that politician was not only in later days to endorse as Minister much of the policy which Peel inaugurated, but was to stand, both as Minister and friend, in an even closer relation to the Queen than Peel himself ever occupied.

III

THE QUEEN AND HER "PERMANENT MINISTER"

STRONG as the mutual feeling undoubtedly was which bound Sir Robert Peel to the Court, it differed in quality from that which the Queen had experienced towards the Minister under whose guidance, as a young and friendless girl, she had assumed her great office. Peel, however, if he had not exactly occupied Lord Melbourne's place, could distinctly claim to have established himself upon a firm and enduring footing in his relation to the Sovereign. To the Queen he was not only a Minister but a friend. When he fell from power, Lord John Russell, who succeeded to his office, did not succeed to the position which he held at Windsor or at Osborne. Owing to the

tact exhibited by the Queen and Prince Albert, there was no very noticeable difference, in so far as the public was concerned, between the place occupied at Court by the new Prime Minister and that which his predecessor had filled. A difference, however, there was, and the finer shades of it appear very clearly by the light of the Queen's journals and the Prince's correspondence. The detachment of the Queen from political partisanship was as complete as ever. As in duty bound, so in reality, her sympathies seemed henceforth always at the command of her Minister, be his colour Whig or Tory. Although the training of a Stockmar may induce in a sovereign absolute loyalty to a political leader who happens to be the servant of the Crown for the time being, it cannot command affection or create intimacy. Neither Lord John Russell nor Lord Derby ever complained of the support accorded to them by the Sovereign. Lord Aberdeen, who had been Foreign Secretary under Peel, and had shared to some extent with him the affectionate esteem of his royal mistress, certainly had no cause to complain, and when he was forced to relinquish his post, even amid the chilly atmosphere of that Crimean winter, the Queen stood almost alone in assuring him of her continued "personal affection and regard." One Minister, it is true, found himself in antagonism to the Crown; but Lord Palmerston's troubles culminated while he still held subordinate, though very high, office; and from the day he became Prime Minister he himself recorded his satisfaction at the "cordiality and confidence" with which he was treated by the Queen.

In point of fact, from the fall of Peel, in 1846, to the fatal 14th of December 1861, the relation between the Sovereign and the Prime Minister was recognised to be wholly different from what it had previously been. A marked and remarkable personality had come between the ruler and the chief of her "confidential servants." During the five years of Sir Robert Peel's Administration, while public attention was fixed on parliamentary conflicts and fiscal changes rousing the wildest animosities, popularly supposed to be pregnant, by enthusiasts of national salvation, and by critics of national ruin, silently and unwatched there was developed an influence which altered fundamentally the whole relation of the Crown to the people, and moulded the Monarchy into the shape which it has now assumed. During those five eventful years the Queen's husband passed from boyhood to manhood, and from prince in name became king in fact. From the moment of her marriage the Queen had recognised, as was natural to a young wife, the intellectual quality of her husband's mind and the moral force of his character.

When she failed to make him King-Consort she was determined that he should not be forced into obscurity. In a most curious memorandum, written by the Queen's own hand, she refers to "Prince George of Denmark, the very stupid and insignificant husband of Queen Anne," who "never seems to have played anything but a very subordinate part" in public affairs; and it is clear that it was not her intention that any such derogatory phrase should ever justly be applied to her own consort. Although the Queen may have believed it to be true that Prince Albert owed his initiation into public life to Sir Robert Peel, in point of fact the Prince was indebted to the Queen herself; for even if Peel was attracted by the ardour and keenness of the young Prince's mind, it never would have occurred to him — fully aware as he was of the political risk he ran—to bring the Prince forward unless he had been conscious that in so doing he was establishing an important hold upon the regard of the Queen. A very acute observer has remarked that before he became her Prime Minister there was probably no man in her dominions whom the Queen so cordially detested as Sir Robert Peel; but that he found means to remove all her prejudice against him, and to establish himself high in her favour; and that when he resigned office the Queen evinced a personal regard for him scarcely inferior to that which she had manifested to Lord Melbourne. At the time it was not so plain as it has since become to what special adroitness Sir Robert Peel owed this remarkable revulsion of feeling on the part of the Queen. It is now clear that it was due to his recognition of Prince Albert as *de facto* coequal sovereign. Lord John Russell was the first with adequate opportunity, as well as sufficient previous experience, to take note of the change which had occurred in the relation of the Sovereign to her Ministers. When he succeeded Sir Robert Peel in office he found that he could no longer expect to see the Queen alone. At every interview between the Sovereign and her Prime Minister the Prince was present. Although, if he had desired to enforce it, Lord John Russell's right to exclude every one from these audiences was incontestable, prudence and tact convinced him at once that the new procedure must be accepted. He stated in confidence to a friend his astonishment at the great development which had taken place. The Prince had become so "identified with the Queen that they were one person"; and it was obvious to him that, while she had the title, he was really discharging the functions of sovereign, and was king to all intents and purposes.

At this time the Prince was in years almost a boy. Although barely six-and-twenty, he seems to have experienced no difficulty in holding his own with Lord John Russell, in spite of the Minister's age and experience, extending over many long years of public life. The qualities to which the Queen had yielded exercised a powerful influence over the minds of all those into whose close companionship, whether for business or pleasure, her husband was thrown. If Sir Robert Peel had been impressed by the young German prince, Lord John Russell and Lord Aberdeen were not less moved by his grave and intense individuality. The effect produced upon successive Ministers by intercourse with him was so marked that groundless suspicions and jealousies, bidding fair to be dangerous, were excited in the minds of politicians who were outside the sphere of his influence. It began to be said that there was a power "behind the throne," and there was but a step between this suggestion and the wilder assertion that this power was used in a sense hostile to the interests of England, and on behalf of foreign States to whom by blood and birth the Prince was more closely allied. From whispers in drawing-rooms and club-windows rumours spread into provincial town-halls and country market-places. Ignited by the public press, suddenly the flames of unpopularity were fanned into a blaze, and Prince Albert became the object, not only of abuse and attack, but also of public impeachment. At one moment it was even credited that he had followed in the wake of former traitors to the State, and had been immured in the Tower. The storm broke, and was allayed in the House of Commons. Then the curious and somewhat unusual spectacle was observed of a Prime Minister, together with his predecessors and successors in that office, agreeing to support each other in an apparently ungrateful cause.

Attempts have been made to analyse the reasons which underlay the Prince's unpopularity. His dress, the cut of his clothes, his manner of shaking hands, his seat on horseback—all these contributed, it was said, to the prejudices of the aristocracy against him. In the *Scotsman* newspaper, in 1854, there appeared an article accounting for the hostility to the young German Prince on the score of his virtues; that as a "moral reformer" he was bound to be obnoxious to all who, "conscious of their own stinted capacities and attainments, tremble for their social position should the lower and middle classes be thoroughly instructed and civilised." By some he was thought a dangerous metaphysician, and by others a prig. His reserve was a standing grievance in higher spheres of society. He was lacking in accustomed freedom and ease of manner; and he never conformed to the ways of the so-called "fast" people in the fashionable world. Above all, he was a "Peelite *malgré lui*," and offended thereby the old-fashioned Tories on the one hand and the advanced section of the Liberal Party on the other. If he was not accused of attempting openly to trench on the privileges of the Sovereign, he was credited with exercising a secret and baneful influence. As he himself put it to the Duke of Wellington, he

> shunned ostentation, and sank his own individual existence in that of his wife; he assumed no separate responsibility before the public, but he became her sole confidential adviser in politics and assistant in communication with the officers of the Government, the father of the royal children, the private secretary of the Sovereign, and her permanent Minister.

Herein lay the gravamen of the charge against him, apparently admitted by himself. A Prime Minister supported by a parliamentary majority had a right to the support and intimate confidence of the Crown, but a "permanent Minister" was a wholly novel and unconstitutional personage. Lord Melbourne had congratulated the Queen on the inestimable advantages she possessed in the counsel and assistance of her husband. Under Peel the Prince's position had become clearer, and he was duly installed as private secretary and intimate "counsellor" of the Queen, taking part in all affairs regarding the Crown or bearing on foreign policy, with the privilege of being present at all audiences between the Sovereign and her Ministers. The internal dissensions of Lord John Russell's Cabinet, the constantly-recurring difficulties with Lord Palmerston, the dismissal of that Minister from the Foreign Office in 1851, and his retirement again in 1853, all contributed to give colour to the reports of unconstitutional interference on the part of the Prince. That his influence, brought to bear upon the vacillating will of Lord John Russell, effected the dismissal of Palmerston in 1851, no one, by the light of documents now revealed in the *Life of the Prince Consort*, can doubt. Lord John Russell's biographer has also, probably with some reluctance, but in the interests of truth, made this plain. Yet, when the debate in Parliament took place in January 1854, in which the attacks on the Prince culminated, no one who had been Prime Minister, or had any hope of becoming so, was found to support the accusation that he had been guilty of the exercise of undue interference. On the contrary, all combined to praise him. Lord Palmerston had, through the Press, already exonerated him by stating that he had exercised "no influence on the Foreign Secretary's resignation and return to office." Lord John Russell and Lord Aberdeen took the whole responsibility of everything that had taken place upon themselves, and bore eloquent witness to the "constitutional action of the Queen." How, they then argued, could the Prince have exercised unconstitutional influence over her, since she herself had not moved a hair's breadth outside the limits of the Constitution? Even Lord Derby, much less well disposed, was driven to speak sharply of the "gullibility of the public" and the "absurd attacks on the Prince." In point of fact, however, the influence of Prince Albert was at this time overwhelming. In March 1851 it was his aversion from Mr. Disraeli, shared by the Queen, that contributed largely to the reluctance of Lord Derby to attempt the formation of a Government, and in all probability prevented him from doing so; and it was the antipathy of the Prince to Lord Palmerston, also shared by the Queen, that procured from Lord John Russell the dismissal of Lord Palmerston in December of the same year.

Even if, as was asserted, Lord Palmerston was addicted to the "monstrous habit of treating with contempt alterations in despatches that had been prescribed to him, and sending despatches from which the Queen and Lord John had struck out certain passages with the same restored," there is no doubt that this habit never galled the Prime Minister to the extent that it annoyed the Prince.

Almost a year before the final rupture with Palmerston the Prince had attempted to sting Lord John Russell into a proper spirit of rebellion against his masterful colleague. On 15th May 1850 he wrote :—

My dear Lord John—Both the Queen and myself are exceedingly sorry at the news your letter conveyed to us. We are not surprised, however, that Lord Palmerston's mode of doing business should not be borne by a susceptible French Government with the same good humour and forbearance as by his colleagues. The Queen hopes to be well enough to see you on Sunday at one o'clock.—Ever yours truly, ALBERT.

Clearly the struggle was not between the Prime Minister and his subordinate. In strength of will and force of character they were too unequally matched. It lay between the subordinate Minister and the "permanent Minister," who was in truth a foeman worthy of Palmerston's steel. It ended, as similar struggles in England nearly always have ended, in the triumph of the subject over the monarch. The biographer of Lord John Russell, who can have had no legitimate bias towards Palmerston, points out that, in spite of the attacks upon his policy and his methods, the victory remained with the Foreign Secretary; and if four years of office had deprived him of the confidence of the Crown, he had gained in exchange for it the confidence of the people. It is to the high credit of the Prince that when Lord Palmerston shortly became, as he was bound to do, the First Minister of the Queen, the relations between him and the Court were no less cordial than those which the Queen had established with his predecessors in office. Although, by offering first Bagshot Park to Lord John Russell, which he refused, and subsequently Pembroke Lodge, which he accepted, the Queen had given evidence of her regard for his upright and loyal nature, the intimacy between her and that Minister was of a different quality from that which had subsisted between her and Sir Robert Peel. To some extent, doubtless, this arose out of the disposition of Lord John Russell himself. Naturally cold in manner, if he took no pains to win goodwill from his followers, he took even less to ingratiate himself in the eyes of one who was not only a sovereign, but a lady. He was the typical leader of that stiff, cold oligarchy which had governed English sovereigns and the English nation by qualities and merits altogether independent of the heart and of the affections.

Next, cool and all unconscious of reproach,
Comes the calm Johnny, who upset the coach.
How formed to lead, if not too proud to please!
His fame would fire you, but his manners freeze.

The Prince, like all men themselves reserved in manner, resented reserve in others. It is clear that to him and to the Queen the sentimental charm of Aberdeen appeared far more attractive than the crude honesty of Russell. As Foreign Secretary in Peel's Government he had been much thrown with the Prince; and Lord Melbourne, soon after his fall, noticed that of the new Ministers Lord Aberdeen was preferred by the Queen.

In December 1852, when Lord Derby resigned, the Queen might have turned quite naturally to Lord John Russell for assistance or advice. He had been her Prime Minister for five years, and no other statesman then living had held that office at all. The Queen, however, sent for Lord Aberdeen and Lord Lansdowne. It is true that at that time, owing to the confusion of parties and the position of the Peelites, the chances of Lord John Russell's forming a Government could have been small; but the opportunity was not given to him. He consented, however, to serve under the Peelite who had been his opponent, just as two years afterwards he consented to serve under the Whig who had been his subordinate almost ten years earlier in his career. In point of fact, while the "permanent Minister" was in the Queen's service the headship of the Cabinet was a matter which seemed to her to affect no one but the rival claimants themselves and their rival ambitions.

From Lord Derby she parted with civility, but without any strong expression of regret. During his ten months of office in 1852, as well as during his year of office in 1858, he enjoyed her friendly but unenthusiastic support. Lord John Russell, thanks to a longer term of official life, and consequently to a larger term of official intercourse, was on terms of somewhat greater cordiality with the Queen. If cold, his deportment to her was always most respectful; he was enough at Court, a cynic observed, to show that he enjoyed the "constitutional confidence of the Sovereign, without being domiciled as a favourite." The extreme levity of Lord Derby, his incapacity for taking grave and serious views, his authority resting altogether, as it did, upon his oratorical gifts, were not likely to endear him to the intense nature of Prince Albert ; and to such a Minister, in the eyes of the Prince, Lord John Russell very greatly, and Lord Aberdeen in an eminent degree, appeared in favourable comparison. Neither of these, however, was to be estimated by the standard of Melbourne, and still less of Peel. There came a time when the Queen, in her "desolate and isolated condition," did indeed turn to "no other than Lord Russell, an old and tried friend of hers," just as there also came a time when Lord Aberdeen was privileged, as he himself relates, to kiss the Queen's hand on saying farewell, and instead of finding it held out in a lifeless manner for the purpose, "to his surprise, when he took hold of it to lift it to his lips, found his own hand squeezed with a strong and significant pressure." This he perhaps rightly interpreted as a proof of real regard ; but, apart from the Minister's queer disclosure, there is evidence in the Queen's own handwriting of her feeling towards him :—

She wishes to say what a pang it is for her to separate from so kind and dear and valued a friend as Lord Aberdeen has ever been to her since she has known him. The day he became her Prime Minister was a very happy one for her; and throughout his Ministry he has ever been the kindest and wisest adviser, one to whom she could apply for advice on all, and trifling occasions even. This she is sure he will still ever be, but the losing him as the first adviser in her Government is very painful.

Considering the circumstances of the parting, amid the frosts and failures of that Crimean winter, and considering the hostile attitude of public opinion towards the Administration of which he was the head, the kindness and warmth of the Queen to a fallen and unpopular servant, though not unusual in her, are none the less worthy of admiration. It will be seen, and easily appreciated, how completely Ministers of this type were dominated and eclipsed in the eyes of the Queen by Prince Albert. Her "permanent Minister" was always about her; and she needed neither the advice nor support of any other. From the fall of Peel, in 1846, to the fall of Aberdeen, in 1855, the Queen looked elsewhere than to her Prime Minister for advice and support. The stronger personality of her husband overshadowed in her eyes the man who happened at the time to be the chief of her "confidential servants."

If by sheer personality the Prince was able to impress a nature so unsympathetic as that of Peel, and influence a man so cold in the ordinary relations of life as Russell, it was not extraordinary that he dominated the mind of her to whom he was a daily, almost an hourly, companion. No woman with any appreciation of intellect, or sensitiveness to character, could fail to be touched by the intense earnestness that breathed through every fibre of his nature. Lady Lyttelton, the governess of the royal children, noticed how this thoroughness of deep feeling permeated through everything that he said or did, even things so trivial as his playing of the organ. It was natural, then, that solemn occasions should have for him a deeper significance than for the majority of young men. The Queen has described how, when he was a little over twenty, he chose to treat the great sacrament of his Church:

The Prince had a very strong feeling about the solemnity of this act, and did not like to appear in company either the evening before or on the day on which he took it, and he and the Queen almost always dined alone on these occasions.

In his ordinary behaviour to the Queen, no less than in his attitude on these graver occasions, it is easy to trace the secret of his power and influence.

He would frequently return to luncheon at a great pace, and would always come through the Queen's dressing-room, where she generally was at that time, with that bright loving smile with which he ever greeted her; telling her where he had been, what new buildings he had seen, what studios, etc., he had visited. Riding for mere riding's sake he disliked, and said *Es ennuyirt mich so.*

It is not surprising that when his life ended, and the loss of her friend, counsellor, and Minister was understood in all its fulness by the Queen, she should have likened it to the "beginning of a new reign." This is, in truth, what it was. From the time of the Queen's illness at the birth of the Princess Royal, when the responsibilities of the Sovereign were undertaken by the Prince, with the tacit approval of the Ministry, to the 14th of December 1861, when his life ended, he was Mayor of the Palace, and all the threads of a constitutional sovereignty were in his hands. The Queen's style is so familiar to the readers of her journals and letters that no one could mistake the source of the communications sent in her name to her Ministers during those years.

Take, for example, the following letter :—

OSBORNE, 10*th March* 1860.

The Queen, in returning Lord Cowley's private letter and secret despatch, agrees with Lord John Russell that he has deserved praise for his mode of answering the Emperor's Napoleonic address.

The circumstance is useful, as proving that the Emperor, if met with firmness, is more likely to retract than if cajoled, and that the statesmen of Europe have much to answer for for having spoiled him in the last ten years by submission and cajolery. The expressions of opinion in the House of Commons have evidently much annoyed the Emperor, but they have also had their effect in making him reflect. If Europe were to stand together, and make an united declaration against the annexation of Savoy, the evil might still be arrested; but less than that will not suffice. The Emperor's last conversation with Lord Cowley is still very vague, leaving him free to do very much what he pleases.

The substance and style of such a letter are unmistakable, and it bears but little resemblance to the memoranda of the Queen which have been quoted. Impressed evidently upon it is the hand of the "permanent Minister," whose authority in Council and weight in argument told heavily in the scale against those of Lord Russell and Lord Aberdeen whenever differences of opinion between the Ministers and the Sovereign arose.

It was only when, in the case of Lord Palmerston, the Prince was brought into collision with a will as strong as his own that anything in the nature of a conflict was sustained; and even then, after a battle in which the spoils of war were fairly divided, the sagacity of the Prince led him to appreciate the force of the statesman with whom he had to deal, and the necessity of compromising their differences. Just as, years before, he had acquiesced in the wisdom of Lord Melbourne's counsel, and had induced the Queen to grant a "general amnesty" in her feelings towards the Tories, so he granted an amnesty to Palmerston, and loyally supported him as First Minister of the Crown.

If, then, the personal relations between the Queen and her Ministers during the full manhood of the Prince were colder and more distant than those which preceded this period, after his death she was once more forced into closer personal intercourse with them, though doubtless of a very different quality.

It is a curious speculation to try and imagine what might have occurred had the Prince Consort lived into late middle age, and into more democratic times. There was nothing in his nature, as it is known to us, which gives the impression that he would have feared democracy. His views were as broad and as elastic as those of Peel. Like Peel's great pupil and follower, whose career has only just ended, the Prince Consort's ideas might easily have kept abreast of the most advanced opinions of the time. Had he lived he would now be ten years the junior of Mr. Gladstone. How, as "permanent Minister," he would have steered through the breakers which beset Lord Beaconsfield's Government in 1879-80, and Mr. Gladstone's in 1884-85, it is impossible to conjecture. Owing to the extreme youth of the Queen the interposition of his strong personality was tolerated for a while. How this interposition would have stood the tension of years may only be conjectured. The eclipse of the constitutional advisers of the Sovereign by a "permanent Minister," even though he be the consort of the Queen, could not fail to be other than an experiment in politics. It must be plain to every one who has carefully noted the inner life of the Palace, as described under the authority of the Queen herself, that it is an experiment which might not safely have been prolonged, and certainly could not safely bear repetition.

IV

THE QUEEN AND LORD PALMERSTON

"Excellent speech of Palmerston's! What a knack he has of falling on his feet! I never will believe after this that there is any scrape out of which his cleverness and good fortune will not extricate him. And I rejoice in his luck most sincerely; for though he now and then trips, he is an excellent minister, and I cannot bear the thought of his being a sacrifice to the spite of other powers." This note, written about 1849, appears in the Journal of Lord Macaulay, who may be said to have possessed a genius for commonplace, and whose views about men and things represented the average of English opinion to a degree unachieved by any contemporary writer.

Lord Macaulay saw with the eyes of the majority of his countrymen, only rather more intently and clearly; and this passage contains the secret of Palmerston's hold upon them. First and foremost he was lucky, and there is, in the view of the average Briton, Cato notwithstanding, no more glorious attribute. Secondly, he was known to be an "excellent minister," free from subtleties, and endowed with a plain understanding, after the manner of a well-to-do citizen. Finally, he was believed to be viewed with jealousy and dislike by all foreigners and in constant danger from their intrigues, sufficient in itself to insure him the highest place in the regard of men who still, like their hero Nelson, had been taught in childhood to "hate a Frenchman as they did the devil."

He was, one of his lifelong opponents said of him after his death, English to the backbone; and he contrived to make Englishmen immeasurably of more account in their own eyes, and to some extent in those of other nations. Palmerston to his contemporaries appeared physically a man of commanding height.

Lord Lorne—his biographer—quotes a description of him, he evidently believing it to be true, in which he is represented as tall and slim. In point of fact he was rather below than above the average height; but a fact of this kind appeared incredible of the Minister who had succeeded in adding a cubit not only to his own moral stature, but to that of the most insignificant of his countrymen. When, after at least ten years of smouldering, the irritation of conscientious colleagues, political foes, and baffled doctrinaires culminated in an attack upon Palmerston in the House of Commons in reference to the treatment of an obscure Greek, the Minister held the House spell-bound from the dusk of one day to the dawn of the next, and, in a speech of extraordinary force from a man who never aspired to rhetoric or even eloquence, reached the zenith of his power and fame. He had confounded his enemies. "It has made us all proud of him," said Sir Robert Peel, addressing the House of Commons for the last time, and the eulogy found a ready echo in the hearts of Englishmen scattered all over the world. If he wished to create, as he declared, a belief that a British subject, in whatever land he may be, shall feel confident in the broad fact of his nationality, that *Civis Romanus sum* was to be the guarantee of every Briton against injustice and wrong, he succeeded beyond his hopes; and so lofty was the spirit he roused, that when for a moment the people believed their favourite Minister to have been false to his own tradition, and to have yielded to the threats of French militarism, they tore his Conspiracy Bill to shreds, and hurled him unceremoniously from power. In spite, however, of this little accident, Lord Palmerston remained for a quarter of a century the most popular of Englishmen in his own country and the most feared abroad. To foreigners generally, and the French in particular, he was—as De Jarnac called him—the incarnation of *La perfide Albion.* Yet the keystone of his foreign policy was a good understanding with France, and it is to the credit of his skill as a Foreign Minister that he was able to maintain the French alliance without for a moment forfeiting the dignity or independence of England as a portion of the price he paid for it. This counted for something among the causes of his popularity. His sympathy, openly expressed, for popular liberties, his dislike and contempt for petty tyranny or oppression, counted for more; while most of all, his cheerful courage in the midst of the difficulties of the Indian Mutiny, and the disasters of the Crimean winter, his never-failing belief that all would be well, and his clear-headed appreciation of what was required, inspired the nation with a confidence that, so long as Palmerston was there, clouds, however black they might appear, would presently disperse.

A final cause, which contributed not a little to the Minister's success, lay in the exaggerations and mouthing of the "Manchester School" of politicians, who, having scored heavily in the fight for Free Trade, had got to believe themselves infallible, and their doctrines only a degree, if at all, less worthy of absolute credence than the Gospels. It had become the fashion with politicians of that school to belittle England, and to obtrude upon the world a cheap cosmopolitanism with an air of superior virtue, extremely galling to men who, either in their own person or by the energy and often by the blood of their sons or brothers, had helped to expand the Empire.

It was only natural that these men—and they formed the large majority—should rally round the Minister who appreciated their sacrifices and took pride in their successes. In politics the law of reaction is well-nigh inexorable, and just as the necessary militarism of the first fifteen years of the century produced the "Manchester School," so that worthy body of doctrinaires was responsible for the ultroneous rule of Palmerston.

A Minister who kept racehorses and had at his command a good store of very blunt vernacular, who could not be got to admit that he understood an abstract thought, who always knew what he wanted and was determined to carry it out regardless of the opinions of others, who conceived his own ideas to be superior to those of other people, who never looked farther than to-morrow, and much preferred not to think beyond this evening, but who at the same time was determined to establish the privilege of an Englishman to the side-walk all over the world, while men of other nations might step into the gutter—this Minister represented aspirations which had long ago sickened under rounded periods intended to convince humanity that bread and calico summed up their total requirements, and were more than sufficient for rational happiness. This was the popular conception of Palmerston when in 1855 he became First Minister of the Crown.

To the Queen he had, for many years, appeared in a somewhat different and less ideal light. There were points in his character which she could not fail to respect and admire, but there was much in his methods as well as in his views which was galling at the time both to her proper pride as Sovereign, and to her dignity as a member of the royal fraternity of Europe. Palmerston had shared the universal admiration excited by the young Queen on her accession. He has left on record his agreeable impressions of her first Council. He was also warmly in favour of her marriage with Prince Albert, and volunteered to Stockmar his opinion that of all possible alliances he chiefly approved the marriage with the Prince. These sentiments were, however, in Palmerston mere platonics, and restrained him not at all from thwarting or from disregarding altogether the ideas of both the Queen and the Prince if they happened to run counter to his own.

To the Prince the character of Palmerston was unsympathetic, and to his speculative mind the positivist Minister was highly uncongenial. Some men, it has been said, think by definition, others by "type." Palmerston never thought otherwise than by "type," and to the Prince he seemed a statesman of a commonplace order, possessing undoubtedly the powers of a first-rate man, but holding the creed of a second-rate man. His frivolity appeared unpardonable in the Germanic eyes of the Prince, and his policy as frivolous and hand-to-mouth as his morals. "When

I was a young man," Palmerston used to say, "the Duke of Wellington made an appointment with me at half-past seven in the morning; and I was asked, 'Why, Palmerston, how will you contrive to keep that engagement?' 'Oh,' I said, 'of course, the easiest thing in the world: I shall keep it the last thing before I go to bed!'" These were not the habits, and badinage was not the tone, of the young Court; so that a fine grain of prejudice hampered the relations between the ebullient Foreign Secretary and his royal mistress. For fifteen years after her marriage, until as her First Minister Palmerston kissed hands in 1855, the friction was constant, and at times paralysing to good government. Opposition only confirmed him in his determination to persevere with a policy, or indulge a freak of temper. In this again he was, as Lord Malmesbury observed, English to the backbone, and in nothing was this characteristic more marked than in his resolve to withstand the influence of the Crown.

If the quarrel—for no other word adequately describes it—between the

Queen and Lord Palmerston originated in the conflicting disposition of her Foreign and her permanent Minister, it shaped itself upon the policy to be pursued in regard to France, and the personal relations existing at the time between the royal families of France and England. With nothing of the doctrinaire about him, Palmerston avoided alliances, and formed his judgment upon questions of foreign policy as they arose. Vaguely he may be said to have desired to keep well with France, but he had given way, as Lord Stratford de Redcliffe remarked, to a strong feeling of resentment against Louis Philippe, and he mistrusted and ultimately detested the whole house of Bourbon. The Prince, on the other hand, full of the great idea of German unity, looked upon France as an enemy to European progress, but was, with the Queen, on terms of intimacy with the King of the French. In 1840, when, by supporting the revolt of Mehemet Ali, France tried to obtain a *quasi* control of Egypt, Palmerston declared "the Mistress of India could not permit France to be mistress directly or indirectly of the road to her Indian dominions." This declaration, since exalted from a platitude into a shibboleth covering the whole "Eastern question," might have obtained the assent of the Queen; but when it was followed by a negotiation with France and Spain relative to the marriages of the Spanish house, culminating in an apparent act of duplicity on the part of Louis Philippe, goaded by an ill-considered despatch of the Foreign Secretary, a state of irritation was engendered between the royal families very painful to the Queen, and laid by her at the door of Lord Palmerston. In her capacity as Sovereign she was stung by the remark that she looked at things *par la lunette* of Palmerston, and although she courageously and loyally supported her Minister's "unfortunate despatch" in her correspondence with the Queen of the French, she did not forgive her Minister for having, as she believed, placed her in a painful predicament.

Between Lord Palmerston and Mr. Gladstone there are not many characteristics in common, but they were alike in the youthful enthusiasm which in old age both statesmen retained. Mr. Motley, describing a party given by Lady Palmerston, uses terms which could now be applied with curious verisimilitude to Mr. and Mrs. Gladstone. In 1848 Lord Palmerston was sixty-four years old, but his enthusiasm for constitutional freedom, not in his own country, where that blessing had long obtained, but in foreign states, was such that in the view of the Queen it induced him to forget that, as England was not prepared to employ force of arms for its achievement, "despatches full of unpleasant truths unpleasantly put could only occasion sore and angry feelings towards this country, without advancing in any degree the cause they were intended to serve."

His creed was the creed of Canning, but his methods were often those of Mrs. Grundy. Occasions were not wanting at that time for the display of his boyish desire to "improve the occasion," and his lectures to foreign rulers gave umbrage in many quarters, and still further widened the breach between the Minister and his Sovereign.

Undoubtedly the tone adopted by Lord Palmerston was often carelessly offensive. "I do not object," said Sir Robert Peel, "to his lordship's giving advice to the Spanish Government, but to his mode of giving it." It was impossible that enthusiasm so exuberant should not occasionally meet with rebuff. On one occasion Spain successfully retorted upon what Peel called the "assumption of superiority" in the style of the Foreign Secretary; while later on, Russia replied in language described by Lord Stanley as "bitter, imperious, and offensive, but not more bitter, more imperious, more offensive, than the provocation." To the Queen these checks to her Minister appeared humiliations, and they were deeply felt and strongly resented. Among her Ministers, as well as among their opponents, she had many sympathisers, and a moment came when Lord John Russell, unable to submit any longer to the haughty deportment of the Foreign Secretary, resolved to retire from the Government. "I feel strongly," he wrote, "that the Queen ought not to be exposed to the enmity of Austria, France, and Russia on account of her Minister." Lord John, however, was mistaken in this assumption, for it was not to the enmity of those nations, but of their rulers, that the Queen was exposed on account of her Foreign Secretary; and in Lord John Russell's confusion lies the justification of Palmerston. The Queen could not be expected to appreciate at the time, for it was far from clear even to Palmerston himself, the service he rendered to the Monarchy in that year of convulsion, when thrones all over Europe were tottering. In 1848 the middle class on the Continent were in open revolt against their rulers. Amid the storms of that year, when no monarch elt secure, Palmerston's "airs of superiority" and his "constitutional lectures" galled intensely, and at no period in history can England have been more cordially detested by neighbouring powers.

To the English middle classes, however, with their ludicrous vanity and pharisaical faith in their own institutions, the attitude of their representative in the Councils of Europe was a keen source of delight. Palmerston's lectures were read and approved with avidity, and while he ministered to the weakness of his countrymen, he fostered in them a wish to maintain their existing constitution intact as an example to other nations of a perfect form of government.

If the Queen had occasion to wince at his methods, she owes largely to Palmerston the ease with which the English monarchy weathered a storm that proved so fatal to other royal houses. His methods were, without question, doubly painful to her ; for not only was the language he employed calculated to embroil her with foreign potentates, with whom she was on terms of friendship, but it frequently happened that over the form of the Palmerstonian philippics she was not permitted to exercise her privilege of imposing a restraining hand. The ostensible cause—if it was not altogether the real one—of the friction which existed for fifteen years between the Sovereign and her

Minister was the careless or studied neglect of the latter to submit his despatches for correction and remark before they were sent to the embassies abroad. As early as 1840 Lord John Russell had complained to Lord Melbourne that he only received "despatches in a printed form some days after they are sent off," and reminded the Prime Minister that in the "days of Lord Grey every important note was carefully revised by and generally submitted to the Cabinet."

Other colleagues of the Foreign Secretary were no less hurt at his high-handed indifference to their opinion. Lord Howick, the late Lord Grey, partly on this ground refused to serve with him, and thus prevented the formation of a Liberal Administration five years later. And eleven years afterwards, in 1851, on this very ground, Lord John Russell when Prime Minister was driven to remove his insubordinate colleague from office altogether. The principle followed by Lord Grey in 1848, when the tension between Palmerston and the Queen became very great, was at the instance of Lord Lansdowne admitted by Palmerston. For although Lord John Russell was Prime Minister, he found it necessary to appeal to Lord Lansdowne to remonstrate with his unruly Foreign Secretary. "The Queen's disapprobation of everything Lord Palmerston does increases," wrote Lady John Russell in her diary at this time; and although Palmerston pretended to believe that the "Queen gave ear too readily to persons hostile to her Government," it is plain that the Prime Minister and the Sovereign were in perfect accord.

In the summer of 1849 a very able State paper was drawn up by the Prince in the name of the Queen, expounding the constitutional rule that the control of foreign policy rests with the Prime Minister, and directing that all despatches submitted for her approval should pass through the hands of Lord John Russell. Whether this was or was not a constitutional rule, Palmerston, although he declared it would "reduce his flint gun to a matchlock," found himself forced to yield, and agreed to alter the existing arrangements in accordance with the Queen's wishes. When the final crisis came, and when after his dismissal from office he had to defend his conduct in Parliament, the Queen's memorandum and his acquiescence in the terms of it were used with damaging effect by Lord John Russell against him. Before, however, the fall of Palmerston, an event had occurred which raised him to the first place in the eyes of his countrymen. This was the attack on his policy in the House of Commons, and his great speech in his own defence. After the Don Pacifico debate, Palmerston became the first of living statesmen in the eyes of the people, a position he never lost till the day of his death fifteen years afterwards. From that time, too, he became more attentive to the wishes of the Queen, although a few months later the old Adam reasserted itself, when over the reception of Kossuth and over the presidential difficulties in France his attitude caused the long-smouldering flame to burst forth. His fall then became inevitable. The *Coup d'État* in France, at once approved by him without consultation with his colleagues, or the knowledge of the Queen, was his *coup de grâce.* "Palmerston is out," wrote Charles Greville, "actually, really, and irretrievably out."

Although the cause was but half guessed at the time, it was known in full to this acute observer and critic. He had watched for some years the widening breach between the Sovereign and her Minister. "As to Palmerston being corrected or reformed, I don't believe a word of it," he had written a year before the crash came, and his prognostication was singularly accurate. He was keenly alive to the dislike of the Court: "The Queen's favourite aversions are: first and foremost Palmerston, and Disraeli next," although the commentator may truly lay stress on the "candid and dispassionate spirit" with which in later years these statesmen were received by their Sovereign. When, however, the tension was greatest, the Queen, acting on the advice of Stockmar, took no active steps to overturn the Foreign Secretary, but allowed the initiative to be taken by Lord John Russell; so that, although for one moment Lord Palmerston may have spoken of a "cabal" against him, his good sense speedily convinced him that he was mistaken, and within a few days of his fall he could speak of the Court without bitterness, and in strong terms could praise the "sagacity of the Queen."

Palmerston's "tit for tat," as he termed it, followed very quickly upon his ejection from office, and when the Government fell he could afford to smile. His triumph over Lord John Russell was complete. Never again was he the subordinate of that statesman in office. The blunders of the Aberdeen Government, of which he was the only popular member, left Lord Palmerston the one indispensable Englishman, and the upshot of his quarrel with the Court and with the leader of the Whigs was to make him the Queen's Prime Minister. Although he was never Foreign Secretary after 1851, his interest in foreign affairs remained undiminished. The Queen has related how when he was Home Secretary in 1853, she, interested in and alarmed about the strikes in the North, put a question to him: "Pray, Lord Palmerston, have you any news?" He replied, "No, madam, I have heard nothing; but it seems certain the Turks have crossed the Danube." Strikes, responsible as he was for order, were as nothing to him compared with the intricacies of the Eastern Question, about which it was not necessary for him specially to concern himself. In 1855, although a futile attempt was made to form an Administration under Lord Granville, in which both Palmerston and Russell were to serve, the universal desire of the nation, supplemented by Lord John's want of tact, placed Lord Palmerston at the head of the Government; and except for a short interval three years later, when his supposed subservience to Napoleon the Third cost him his office, Prime Minister he remained until his death ten years afterwards.

From the moment he became her First Minister his position relative to the Queen underwent a marked change. Lord Aberdeen, who was on friendly terms with the Prince, said to Bishop Wilberforce, a few months after Palmerston's accession to office, that "the Queen has not altered at all in her real feelings to him. She behaves perfectly well and truly to him. It has always been her great virtue, but she does not like him a bit better than she did, nor the Prince either." If this was the case, there is no corroboration of it, and indeed all the evidence points to the gradual arriving at a perfectly good understanding with both the Queen and the Prince. The causes of difference had indeed passed away. No doubt the Prince still found much which was unsympathetic to him in Palmerston's character. Although he could admire, as every one did, the great physical vigour of a Prime Minister who, when seventy years old, could row on the Thames before breakfast, or swim in the river like an Eton boy, or who, when nearly eighty, was able to ride from London to Harrow and back in one day, yet he shrank from what Lord Houghton called "Palmerston's ha-ha and *laissez-faire*." The Prime Minister's ethical views amused the maids-of-honour, and made them laugh, but they seemed drearily inadequate to the grave-minded Prince. When, however, the fatal

December of 1861 crushed the Queen's life, Lord Palmerston was the first to realise the irreparable loss which, as wife and Sovereign, she had sustained, and to appreciate her meaning when she spoke of having to "begin a new reign."

For many years before the Prince's death, he and Palmerston had worked well together. Their struggle had ended in 1855, when Palmerston became Prime Minister. While the Prince had contended for a constitutional punctilio, Palmerston had fought for his own hand. It was not on principle that he objected to the control by the Prime Minister and the Crown over the Foreign Secretary; his objections were founded on the circumstance that he himself was the Foreign Secretary it was proposed to control. Of late years, owing to the accident of Lord Salisbury combining the office of Foreign Secretary and Prime Minister, the desirability of having two heads instead of one to manage the foreign relations of the country has been erected into a principle. The afterthought sprang in the usual way from the spirit of opposition, and not from any rational or careful consideration of the question based on experience. Those, however, who denounced Lord Salisbury must recognise the force of the Queen's contention in her struggle with Palmerston, and her celebrated memorandum must to them appear the charter of Foreign Office subservience. In reality the temper of the Foreign Secretary is the key of the situation. Given a man full of restless activity and hasty enthusiasms, then the mere time involved in sending despatches in red boxes to the Queen is so much gained for reflection. Given a minister of a calmer type, control or supervision is only a work of supererogation, and frequently a fatal loss of the psychological moment. When the Queen was engaged in endeavouring to check the youthful ardour of Lord Palmerston, she was little more than a girl in years, while he was well beyond the farthest limit of middle age. Yet in many ways he was incomparably the younger of the two. To the Queen supreme responsibility came early in life, and, as usual, it aged her; while to Palmerston supreme responsibility came late, and found him still a boy in mind. He was fifty years in the House of Commons before he led that assembly; and during that half-century, although constantly in office, he had not been a regular speaker or even a regular attendant in the House. "I can't get that three-decker Palmerston to bear down," Mr. Canning used to say; and Palmerston always hesitated to formulate views upon any subject which was not his special care at the moment. He refused to set his mind to work up hypotheses. In fact, he was a typical man of the world, and, as it has been often said, a man of the world is not an imaginative animal. When Lord Houghton found himself next to Mr. Gladstone at dinner half-a-century ago, he found him "excited about China and the cattle-plague, and half-a-dozen other things"; when he found himself next to Lord Palmerston he could get no farther than the inevitable ha-ha and *laissez-faire*. What was admirable, however, in Lord Palmerston, was his ever-present sense of the dignity of England. "Tell M. Guizot from me," said Metternich, "that one does not with impunity play little tricks with great countries." Lord Palmerston never stooped to little tricks himself, and would not tolerate them in others. This attitude, together with his firmness about the military forces of the Crown and his cheerful confidence in the fortune and stamina of his countrymen in 1853 and 1857, was thoroughly appreciated by the Queen; so that when the end came she could look back and mourn honestly at the breaking of "another link of the past," and feel sincerely and "deeply in her desolate and isolated condition how one by one those tried servants and advisers are taken from her." As befitted him, Lord Palmerston died in harness. Realistic and Hellenic in spirit as he was, like his prototype of old who kept a bow which he strung daily to test his failing strength, the Prime Minister within a few weeks of his death was seen to come out of the house at Brocket, look lest he was observed, and then slowly and deliberately climb an iron railing as a test of his bodily vigour. He was over fourscore, and death took him quickly and kindly while still in full possession of his faculties and still in the plenitude of power. Four years before he died, the Queen must have felt that her life had ended. Yet it is now a generation since Lord Palmerston's death, and the Queen, to whose sagacity he bore witness so long ago, still sagaciously rules the nation that he helped to make great. As the first portion of her reign may be said to have synchronised with the fall of Peel, so the second portion ended with the death of Palmerston. Henceforth she was destined to be thrown with a new generation of public servants, men well known to her by name and fame, some of whom had already served her in positions of responsibility, but none of whom had passed in close relation with her through the excitements of her queenship, and the joys and sorrows of her married life. In spite of differences and quarrels, the Queen had always extended to Lord Palmerston that straightforward support of the lack of which none of her Ministers have ever complained, and when he died she could not help feeling that her youth had passed away with him, and that she was left a lonely woman face to face with the awful responsibilities of her great office, without one human being in the world whom she could call an old friend.

V

THE QUEEN AND LORD BEACONSFIELD

On the wall of Hughenden Church may be seen a memorial tablet, recording the gratitude and affection of Queen Victoria for the services and for the memory of a man who without question was the most interesting and striking figure of her reign. The inscription which it bears was written by the Queen herself. "To the dear and honoured memory," so it runs, "of Benjamin, Earl of Beaconsfield, this memorial is placed by his grateful and affectionate Sovereign and friend, Victoria R.I. 'Kings love him that speaketh right.'—Prov. xvi. 13." This inscription is in many ways noteworthy. To find a memorial erected by a sovereign to a subject is in itself sufficiently remarkable, but so rare an act of condescension is unique coupled with public expressions of gratitude and friendship.

These qualities are not common in kings accustomed to accept devotion or service as their due, and even from Queen Victoria such strong words read strangely when it is remembered that they are from the hand of a Queen of England towards one whom her ancestors would have scorned as the son of a hated and despised race, whom to this day some of her relatives and regal cousins hound and persecute with all the unenlightened fervour of the middle ages. It was meet, however, that in a Christian church such a memorial, raised by the supreme head of that Church, to a Jew by blood and by every fibre of his nature, should be rounded off by a quotation from the proverbial philosophy of the most famous ruler of his race, and fitter still that there should be found affixed to it a signature, the novelty of which to English eyes recalls the fact that Lord Beaconsfield aspired to rank with Bismarck and Cavour as the consolidator of Imperial rule.

If in politics an opportunist, in character no man could have exhibited greater consistency throughout a long life; and that Lord Beaconsfield should lie, not in Westminster Abbey surrounded by the ashes of the "Venetian party," but among the villagers of a Buckinghamshire hamlet, under a memorial raised to him by the occupant of the Throne, was a fit climax to the creed he professed in youth, and carried with him to almost supreme power, and to the grave. If he began political life amid the contemptuous jeers of a Tory House of Commons, he lived to receive the profound adulation and enjoy the absolute confidence of the Conservative party. If the first thirty years of his political existence were passed in the cold shadow of royal disapprobation and dislike, he lived to become the darling of the Court and to earn the inscription which adorns his tomb. These variations of sentiment were in no way due to changes in Disraeli himself, but rather to the slow appreciation by others of his rare personality. His character never underwent any marked development, while the ideas which well-nigh choked his youth found expression in maturity and old age. In his political enthusiasms and hatreds he was alike consistent and persevering. No one ever suspected him of a weakness for the Whigs whom he hated, nor doubted his sympathy for the people whom he trusted, and his regard for the Throne which he upheld. As a Tory Democrat he appeared an abnormal growth to the "sublime mediocrity" of Peel and of his party, yet he lived to establish household suffrage and to convert the diadem of the English kings into an Imperial crown.

In youth Disraeli brooded over problems of statecraft, and these very problems he lived largely to solve as a Minister. To those who read his political tracts, cast by him into the original form of the political novel, and who were familiar with his foppish appearance and his florid style of speech, it appeared impossible that he should figure in any other character than that of the political charlatan and social buffoon. Yet over these prejudices, permanent in some minds, completely overcome in others,

Disraeli triumphed by sheer force of talent and energy. With the dawn of a new era in English politics, in 1832, his strenuous public life began; and when, half-a-century later, he had had his fill of life and honour, men began to appreciate how full the intervening years had been of indomitable strife, devoted to the gradual conquest of the ear of the House of Commons, of the confidence of the Conservative party, of the goodwill of the Sovereign, and of the support of the nation. All these were finally won, and this extraordinary child of Israel, whose ancestors were unhappy refugees hunted from Spain to Venice, whose immediate forebears were poor immigrants into a London suburb, sat himself down in the seat of the chief of the House of Stanley, dictated his will to the proudest aristocracy on earth, posed as the representative of the English race among the assembled Powers of Europe, took Great Britain into the hollow of his hand, clothed a *nation boutiquière* with Imperial purple, left behind him a cause identified with his name, and a party strong enough to defend it, and finally sank into a grave smothered with flowers by the hands of the people, and surmounted by a memorial inscribed by the hand of the Queen. The Napoleonic era of marvels furnishes no example more romantic of the triumph of individual capacity over hostile conditions.

Although much has been made by political adversaries of the flattery by which Lord Beaconsfield is supposed to have influenced the Queen, there is not a scrap of evidence to show that in his relations with the Sovereign he employed arts or adopted methods foreign to those used by Lord Aberdeen or by Sir Robert Peel. The secret of his success lay not in subservience to the will of the monarch, but in masculine appreciation of her sex. It is noteworthy that among all his personal triumphs that over the Queen was the longest deferred. In 1852, when he took office as Chancellor of the Exchequer, his position as leader of the House of Commons was assured. Yet it was with reluctance that the Conservative party, under severe pressure from its chief, yielded to his leadership, and even as late as 1867 powerful Tory peers, like Lord Lonsdale, were known to doubt whether Disraeli would ever be loyally accepted by the party in succession to Lord Derby as their head. That the English people were far from placing trust in him was clear from the minority in which for twenty-two years they left his following in Parliament; and it was well known that in his office of Chancellor of the Exchequer he had been unwillingly approved by the Queen, so violent was her prejudice against him, mainly on the ground that the holder of that office was not brought into personal contact with the Sovereign. By 1874 the English people had been won over, and Mr. Disraeli was at last, after a prolonged and patient novitiate, entrusted with a large majority in the House of Commons. Thenceforth his task was easy, and the entire confidence of his party was his reward for the triumph they owed to his adroit leadership. Mr. Disraeli then stepped from the ranks of clever politicians, and took his place among European statesmen. It was at this time that the last barrier between the Prime Minister and the Queen fell to the ground. Dislike, dating from a time when Disraeli's bitter invective was goading to fury Sir Robert Peel's friends, and among them the Sovereign, had long since given way; but only half confidence had supervened, bred of mistrust in the alien and too nimble politician. Now this in turn was swept aside, and Lord Beaconsfield filled the place so long left vacant, and became the "friend" of the Queen as well as First Minister of the Crown.

Antipathies, to a far greater extent than is generally supposed, have a physical basis, and although Disraeli in youth possessed a certain weird beauty, it was of a kind unlikely to attract favourably either men or women of a northern race. When he first rose to address the House of Commons on the 7th of December 1837, he was

very showily attired, being dressed in a bottle-green frock-coat and a waistcoat of white, of the Dick Swiveller pattern, the front of which exhibited a network of glittering chains; large fancy-pattern pantaloons, and a black tie, above which no shirt collar was visible, completed the outward man. A countenance lividly pale, set out by a pair of intensely black eyes and a broad but not very high forehead overhung by clustered ringlets of coal-black hair, which, combed away from the right temple, fell in bunches of well-oiled small ringlets over his left cheek.

Then, again, his manner of speaking was not that to which the House of Commons was accustomed. He is thus described by an eye-witness :—

His gestures were abundant: he often appeared as if trying with what celerity he could move his body from one side to another, and throw his hands out and draw them in again. At other times he flourished one hand before his face, and then the other. His voice, too, is of a very unusual kind: it is powerful, and had every justice done to it in the way of exercise; but there is something peculiar in it which I am at a loss to characterise. His utterance is rapid, and he never seemed at a loss for words. On the whole, and notwithstanding the result of his first attempt, I am convinced he is a man who possesses many of the requisites of a good debater. That he is a man of great literary talent few will dispute.

To eyes by long usage inclined to gauge a man by the symmetry of his top boots and the stains on his hunting coat, or, as in the case of Castlereagh or Althorp, to trust an orator in inverse ratio to his intelligibility, Disraeli seemed untrustworthy and dangerous. Sober men, too, looked askance at this foreign-looking person who could fashion an epigram as readily as they could knock over a cock pheasant. Even so cosmopolitan a bishop as Wilberforce, though he was fascinated, could not recognise in him a countryman. "I enjoyed meeting Disraeli," he wrote as late as 1867. "He is a marvellous man. Not a bit a Briton, but all over an Eastern Jew; but very interesting to talk to." Yet this was thirty years later than that famous first appearance in Parliament, which had provoked alike uproarious mirth from an undiscriminating assembly, and the well-remembered threat from its victim that a day would come when they would be forced to give him a hearing.

Certainly, when Bishop Wilberforce wrote, the time had long passed when Disraeli had need to crave a hearing from the House of Commons. In 1852 his "pre-eminence in opposition had given him an indisputable title" to the leadership of that assembly; but, strangely enough, popularity had not accrued to him with power. Four years later his titular leader, Lord Derby, writing to Lord Malmesbury, observed: "As to Disraeli's unpopularity, I see it and regret it, and especially regret that he does not see more of his party in private; but they could not do without him, even if there were any one ready and willing to take his place." Personal contact, according to this practised and shrewd observer, was the cure for the vehement prejudices of his party against their abnormal political chief. "Disraeli has no influence in the country," observed Greville, about this time, "and a very doubtful position in his own party." Yet personal contact rarely triumphs over prejudice, and proverbially seldom strengthens respect unless the latent qualities in a man are of the loftiest order. That this was the case with Mr. Disraeli seems not improbable, for certain it is that his foes were chiefly to be found among those to whom personally he was unknown, while few men have been so well served and so well liked by those with whom he desired and claimed intercourse.

In the early years of her reign the Queen can have heard but little of Disraeli. Although the chief of the Young England party, and the author of novels that had a certain vogue, he and his following were not at that time a serious factor in politics. To Disraeli, however, to his romantic fondness for women, and to his reverence for the stately aspect of the Throne, the Queen's personality already strongly appealed. Had he not felt strongly the charm before which Lord Melbourne and Peel succumbed, the celebrated passage in *Sybil* could not have been written :—

Hark ! it tolls ! All is over. The great bell of the metropolitan cathedral announces the death of the last son of George the Third who probably will ever reign in England. He was a good man : with feelings and sympathies ; deficient in culture rather than ability ; with a sense of duty ; and with something of the conception of what should be the character of an English monarch. Peace to his manes !

We are summoned to a different scene.

In a palace in a garden, not in a haughty keep, proud with the fame but dark with the violence of ages; not in a regal pile, bright with the splendour, but soiled with the intrigues of courts and factions; in a palace in a garden, meet scene for youth, and innocence, and beauty, came a voice that told the maiden that she must ascend her throne!

The Council of England is summoned for the first time within her bowers. There are assembled the prelates and captains and chief men of her realm; the priests of the religion that consoles, the heroes of the sword that has conquered, the votaries of the craft that has decided the fate of empires; men grey with thought, and fame, and age; who are the stewards of divine mysteries, who have toiled in secret cabinets, who have encountered in battle the hosts of Europe, who have struggled in the less merciful strife of aspiring senates; men, too, some of them, lords of a thousand vassals and chief proprietors of provinces, yet not one of them whose heart does not at this moment tremble as he awaits the first presence of the maiden who must now ascend her throne.

A hum of half-suppressed conversation, which would attempt to conceal the excitement which some of the greatest of them have since acknowledged, fills that brilliant assemblage; the sea of plumes, and glittering stars, and gorgeous dresses. Hush! the portals open; she comes; the silence is as deep as that of a noontide forest. Attended for a moment by her royal mother and the ladies of her court, who bow and then retire, VICTORIA ascends her throne; a girl, alone, and for the first time, amid an assemblage of men.

In a sweet thrilling voice, and with a composed mien which indicates rather the absorbing sense of august duty than an absence of emotion, THE QUEEN announces her accession to the throne of her ancestors, and her humble hope that divine Providence will guard over the fulfilment of her lofty trust.

The prelates and captains and chief men of her realm then advance to the throne, and, kneeling before her, pledge their troth, and take the sacred oaths of allegiance and supremacy.

Allegiance to one who rules over the land that the great Macedonian could not conquer; and over a continent of which even Columbus never dreamed; to the Queen of every sea, and of nations in every zone.

It is not of these that I would speak; but of a nation nearer her footstool, and which at the moment looks to her with anxiety, with affection, perhaps with hope. Fair and serene, she has the blood and beauty of the Saxon. Will it be her proud destiny at length to bear relief to suffering millions, and, with that soft hand which might inspire troubadours and guerdon knights, break the last links in the chain of a Saxon thraldom?

It was in 1845 that *Sybil* was published, a year fertile with events which for the first time brought Mr. Disraeli prominently to the notice of the Queen and of the Prince Consort, and to which may be traced a hostile prejudice lasting in the case of the Prince till his death, and in the mind of the Queen for the space of a generation.

His attacks on Sir Robert Peel, virulent and unrelenting, were looked upon by the Sovereign, not as the legitimate assault by one political opponent upon another, but as the stroke of an assassin at the heart of a friend. The whole nature of the Prince, his sanity and love of sober discussion, his loyalty and respect for character, his economic mind and hatred of claptrap, revolted against the Protectionist Ahithophel. To his Teutonic eyes Peel was the noble, broad-minded English gentleman, slowly beaten down by the arts of this Satanic Jew. It was a sentiment widely shared even by those glad to make use of any stick, effectually tempered, with which to beat one whom they feared as a despoiler and branded as a traitor. The Queen shared the Prince's views, and when, six years later, she was obliged to receive Mr. Disraeli as a Minister, her reluctance was well known and secretly condoned by her subjects. "Make them fear you, and they will kiss your feet," said some one to Vivian Grey; and Disraeli invariably took his own sermons to heart. He had made the House of Commons fear him, and the House of Commons accepted the "smile for a friend and the sneer for the world" with which he enforced his rule. That he, like his colleague George Smythe, could prove a splendid failure he was determined should not be; and the obstacles which hitherto had yielded to his untiring courage he was resolved should be surmounted to the last.

"The only power," said Coningsby, "that has no class sympathy is the Sovereign"; and this thesis he was bent on proving, in spite of the Sovereign herself. It was a question of perseverance, high daring, and time. To him, a son of patriarchs whose span of life was counted by centuries, the flight of time appeared a small factor. He was never hurried. It seemed as if he, too, one of the chosen people, might expect to live beyond the ordinary term of man's life. After twenty years of strife for the lead of the House of Commons, he, an alien, was at length the first man in that proud assembly. He could well wait, if necessary, twenty more for the confidence of the English people and that of their Sovereign.

With marvellous endurance and patient tenacity—those heroic qualities of his race—he waited; and he had his reward. "The most wonderful thing," wrote Bishop Wilberforce, not a friendly witness, "is the rise of Disraeli. It is not the mere assertion of talent, as you hear so many say. It seems to me quite beside that. He has been able to teach the House of Commons almost to ignore Gladstone, and at present lords it over him."

It was to certain great qualities of character, as extraordinary as his intellectual powers, that Mr. Gladstone himself bore witness in asking the House of Commons to vote a public monument to Lord Beaconsfield. These were his strong will, his long-sighted persistency of purpose, his remarkable power of self-government, and last, not least, his great parliamentary courage. "I have known," said Mr. Gladstone, "some score of Ministers, but never any two who were his equal in these respects."

Had the Prince Consort lived, regard on his side must have followed the inevitable intimacy into which the two men were thrown. To Mr. Disraeli the Prince's qualities were apparent from the first. Although in 1854, when jealousy of the Prince's position near the Queen culminated in an attack upon him in Parliament, Disraeli remained silent, he had written only a few days before a strong expression of favourable opinion. "The opportunity," he says, "which office has afforded me of becoming acquainted with the Prince filled me with a sentiment towards him which I may describe, without exaggeration, as one of affection." That the feeling was far from reciprocal is well known. The Prince's was not a nature to be taken by storm. That he would have yielded, as the Queen yielded ultimately, to the firm pressure of a powerful character no one can reasonably doubt. Partisanship has invested Lord Beaconsfield in later days with the attributes of those artful men who, as it has been said, study the passions of princes and conceal their own, in order to acquire and retain influence. If Lord Beaconsfield, in his dealings with the Sovereign, stooped to the employment of arts, they were of the simplest kind. He once described his method to a friend. "I never contradict," he said; "I never deny; but I sometimes forget." To the bore or the Pharisee such maxims may seem degrading; but there is many a man, under the pressure of ministerial or domestic sufferings, who will envy the serene philosophy of Lord Beaconsfield.

Chance is often the determining factor in our likes and dislikes; and it so happened that the year 1874, which gave Mr. Disraeli his majority, establishing him a second time Prime Minister, was psychologically favourable to his influence at Court. His first administration, seven years before, extending over a few months only, had given him inadequate opportunity. Now his personal magnetism could be employed under circumstances altogether favourable. The Queen had been engaged for some time in the heart-stirring task of reconstructing for the perusal of her people the *Life of the Prince Consort.* To contemplate old journals and letters, to permit the past to invade the present, to revive the memory of youth and friends long dead, is to open the heart and mind to new and kindling impressions. The Queen was enabled to realise afresh how much she had lost. Of the friends of her girlhood not one remained; and of those who had stood near the throne during her early married life, Lord Russell alone was left—already in the half-shadow of death. Almost the last link with the past snapped by the death in May 1874 of M. Van de Weyer, who had been the friend of her uncle King Leopold, and had received a large and intimate share of the confidence of the Queen. For reasons, some obvious and some obscure, Mr. Gladstone followed rather in the steps of Palmerston and Derby than those of Aberdeen and Peel, whom in character he far more closely resembled. Certain it is that his relation to the Queen, though it may have been that of a trusted Minister, was not that of a friend. Mr. Disraeli succeeded, however, in reinspiring sentiments which had for long lain dormant; and once more in the old place occupied by Lord Melbourne in her charming and helpless girlhood, before the days when she could look to her permanent Minister for guidance, there stood a Minister who was at once the Queen's constitutional adviser and her private friend.

Disraeli's chivalrous devotion to women is abundantly clear from his novels, but it has been made clearer still to those, Mr. Froude among them, who have had access to his unpublished letters to Mrs. Brydges Williams in the library at Tring Park, and who were cognisant of his almost daily correspondence with another lady of great powers of mind and personal charm, who, to the deep sorrow of all who knew her, has recently followed the leader whom she honoured with her friendship. His loyal devotion to Lady

Beaconsfield and the adoration he inspired in her have for long been notorious. What wonder, then, that to Disraeli, a romanticist in statecraft, an idealist in politics, and a Provençal in sentiment, his chivalrous regard for the sex should have taken a deeper complexion when the personage was not only a woman but a queen? In trifles Disraeli never forgot the sex of the Sovereign. In great affairs he never appeared to remember it. To this extent the charge of flattery brought against him may be true. He approached the Queen with the supreme tact of a man of the world, than which no form of flattery can be more effective and more dangerous. So far the indictment against him may be upheld. The word "subservience" is the translation of this simple fact into the language of political malice. It has been freely used, and events of such vast import as the Imperial Title and the Congress of Berlin were put down by political adversaries to the flexibility of the courtier rather than to the supreme volition of the statesman. If it was true of Charles Earl Grey that he

Wrought in brave old age what youth had
planned,

it was equally true of Lord Beaconsfield. It was noticed that he had always a fantastic taste for the outward and visible side of a cause or of an idea, and the Imperial notion in *Tancred* readily took the shape of the Imperial Titles Bill. There is a passage in this novel, written thirty years before the Queen assumed the title of Empress of India, before the first use outside India of Indian troops in Imperial interests, and before the hold of England upon Alexandria was obtained by the purchase for four millions of the Khedive's shares in the Suez Canal. It runs thus:—

You must perform the Portuguese scheme on a great scale; quit a petty and exhausted position for a vast and prolific empire. Let the Queen of the English collect a great fleet, let her stow away all her treasure, bullion, gold plate, and precious arms; be accompanied by all her Court and chief people, and transfer the seat of her empire from London to Delhi. There she will find an immense empire ready made, a first-rate army, and a large revenue. . . . I will take care of Syria and Asia Minor. The only way to manage the Afghans is by

Persia and by the Arabs. We will acknowledge the Empress of India as our suzerain, and secure for her the Levantine coast. If she like, she shall have Alexandria as she now has Malta: it could be arranged. Your Queen is young; she has an *avenir*. Aberdeen and Sir Peel will never give her this advice; their habits are formed; they are too old, too *rusés*. But, you see! the greatest empire that ever existed; besides which she gets rid of the embarrassment of her Chambers! And quite practicable; for the only difficult part, the conquest of India, which baffled Alexander, is all done!

Looking at the dreams of Mr. Disraeli in 1847, and the achievements of Lord Beaconsfield in 1877, it is scarcely a matter of surprise that the Queen of England, who cannot fail to appreciate, in keen personal degree, the glorification of British authority over the world, should yield willingly her favour and support such a Minister. It was not difficult for the Queen, when she appeared to maintain her own will, to be found in reality carrying out that of her Imperial Chancellor. "I had to prepare the mind of the country," Mr. Disraeli once said, "to educate—if it be not too arrogant to use such a phrase—to educate our party." He did in truth educate, not only his party but his countrymen at large, and finally the Sovereign. His party he converted to that form of Tory Democracy which sanctioned the Reform Bill of 1867. His countrymen he converted from "a nation of shopkeepers" into Rhodesian Imperialists, and inflicted a mortal wound upon the Manchester School. The Queen he converted from a Whig Sovereign into the Empress of India. It was the spirit of the age, he would himself have said, which he did no more than interpret. A cool and friendly foreign critic said of England in the early seventies that she had "fallen into disrepute among nations," and that the fate of Holland was everywhere foretold for her. England with her teeming millions, requiring more than ever an outlet into fresh lands for her people, and new markets for her commerce, may have grown restive under this dangerous and unworthy suspicion. Lord Beaconsfield may have done no more than follow the example of Sir Robert Peel in 1846, and gauge accurately the poignant necessities of the epoch over which he was called upon to preside. It is impossible to deny to him the attribute of rare political insight. When in March 1873 he refused to take office, but declared nevertheless that the Tory party then occupied the "most satisfactory position which it has held since the days of its greatest statesmen, Mr. Pitt and Lord Grenville"; that it had "divested itself of those excrescences which are not indigenous to its native growth, but which in a time of long prosperity were the consequence sometimes of negligence, and sometimes, perhaps, in a certain degree, of ignorance"; although his political adversaries laughed, within a year Mr. Disraeli had the laugh on his side, and what he called the "career of plundering and blundering" on the part of the Liberal party had come to a disastrous end. As the shadows gathered round him, the love of prophecy, deep-seated in his race, often gleamed out. In 1880 he said to a friend, "I give myself two years more of life." To the Queen he gave twenty. Not long before he had penned his famous letter to the Duke of Marlborough. No manifesto was ever more criticised, and even his warmest friends cavilled at the prophetic allusions to the adoption of Home Rule by his political adversaries. It was indeed early days to speak of the party then led by Lord Hartington as being "ready to challenge the imperial character of the realm"; as a party that, having "failed to enfeeble the colonies by their policy of decomposition, may perhaps now recognise in the disintegration of the United Kingdom a mode which will not only accomplish but precipitate their purpose." The phrases are those of a hostile parliamentary critic, but the prescience is that of a statesman or a prophet.

The Queen parted from her Minister with unfeigned sorrow. On this man who had complained that all existence was an ennui or an anxiety, but who nevertheless said of his dying wife, "for thirty-three years she has never given me a dull moment," this man who was accused by his friends of taciturnity, who was but twice seen to laugh, and who "kept all his fireworks for when women were present," the Queen had bestowed that strong regard which had not been given to any Prime Minister since Lord Aberdeen. Honours for himself, an earldom, the Garter, honours for his friends, all these things were nothing. They were the due of any Minister who chose to press for them. The "affection and friendship" of the Sovereign could not be claimed as a right. They had no necessary place in a Prime Minister's gazette. If the Queen chose to visit Hughenden, and walk on the south terrace among her Minister's peacocks, much as years before she had visited Drayton, her line of Ministers between Peel and Lord Beaconsfield had no legitimate cause of complaint. Like Mordecai, he was the man whom the Sovereign delighted to honour.

"Attended this week the opening of Parliament," writes Archbishop Tait in his Journal of 1877—

the Queen being present and wearing for the first time, some one says, her crown as Empress of India. Lord Beaconsfield was on her left side, holding aloft the sword of state. At five the House again crammed to see him take his seat; and Slingsby Bethell, equal to the occasion, read aloud the writ in very distinct tones. All seemed to be founded on the model, "What shall be done to the man whom the king delighteth to honour?"

It was exactly forty years, that mystic number of the Jewish race, from the day when the newly-elected member for Shrewsbury had taken his seat for the first time in the House of Commons. Then, despised as a clever, unscrupulous dandy, jeered at as a fop who had mistaken his vocation, hanging on to the skirts of Lord Lyndhurst with one hand and those of Lady Blessington with the other, he seemed destined to perpetual failure. Now, standing on the left side of the Queen, bearing aloft the sword of state, an Earl and First Minister of the Crown, the most conspicuous figure at that moment in Europe, he had achieved the wildest improbabilities of which his romantic youth had dreamed. A few years more, and he was back at Hughenden, a broken, dying man, whose web of life was woven at last, spending months in absolute solitude, with only the shadows of the past about him. "'Dreams! dreams! dreams!' he murmured as he gazed into the fire," records a visitor to Hughenden, and they had been in truth the staple of his life. Mr. Disraeli as a novelist—a dreamer of dreams—had preceded Mr. Disraeli the politician. Lord Beaconsfield as a novelist survived Lord Beaconsfield the statesman. *Vivian Grey* and *Endymion*—they mark the beginning and the end. To the "dear and honoured memory" of this extraordinary man his Sovereign inscribed her gratitude and affection. Perhaps to such feelings as these, ever inspired in those nearest to him, may be attributed the secret of his triumph over conditions apparently so hostile.

That Lord Beaconsfield's character presented aspects repellent to the political purists cannot be questioned; and that politics were oftener than not to him a game or a fine piece of strategy rather than a conflict of principle must be unquestioned. It is perhaps not doubtful that he feigned some sentiments he was far from feeling, and masked others that he felt deeply. The dictum that far-reaching ambition and perfect scrupulousness can hardly coexist in the same mind he perhaps exemplified. By the Queen this incompatibility was noticed, when it was indeed painfully obvious, and she shrank from the spectacle. As years rolled on, the conflict grew less glaring, and the Queen's attention, together with that of her subjects, became fixed on the finer qualities of the man. His pertinacity and undaunted courage, his patience under obloquy, his untiring energy, his high conception of the honour and keen regard for the interests of England—all these characteristics were recognised and admired. There was one quality, however, which is rare in statesmen, and even if present is not always patent to the world. In a leader of men it is the key to success, and in an aspirant to fame the secret of power. Dizzy, as he was for so long affectionately called, possessed the inestimable quality of perfect loyalty to his friends. He was never known to forget a kindness or ignore a service. He was never suspected of having betrayed a follower or forgotten a partisan. However irritating the blunder, however black the catastrophe, Mr. Disraeli could be relied on in the hour of need. His personal hatreds were well under control—"I never trouble to be avenged," he once said to the writer; "when a man injures me I put his name on a slip of paper and lock it up in a drawer. It is marvellous how men I have thus labelled have the knack of disappearing!" In judging men, though not infallible, he seldom erred. Among his opponents, long before they had made a mark, he noticed Lord Rosebery and Sir William Harcourt. The former he took some pains to attract. Of the latter he said, "He is the only man in the House, except myself, who knows the history of his country." When Lord Hartington was making his first speech in Parliament, Mr. Disraeli turned to the colleague sitting next him and murmured, "This young man will do." Among his friends he showed equal discrimination. His reliance upon Lord Cairns, the most powerful and courageous intellect in the

Cabinet of 1874, was absolute; and during his absence at the Congress of Berlin it was to the Chancellor that he very wisely looked to sustain the burden of Government at home. He appointed [redacted]

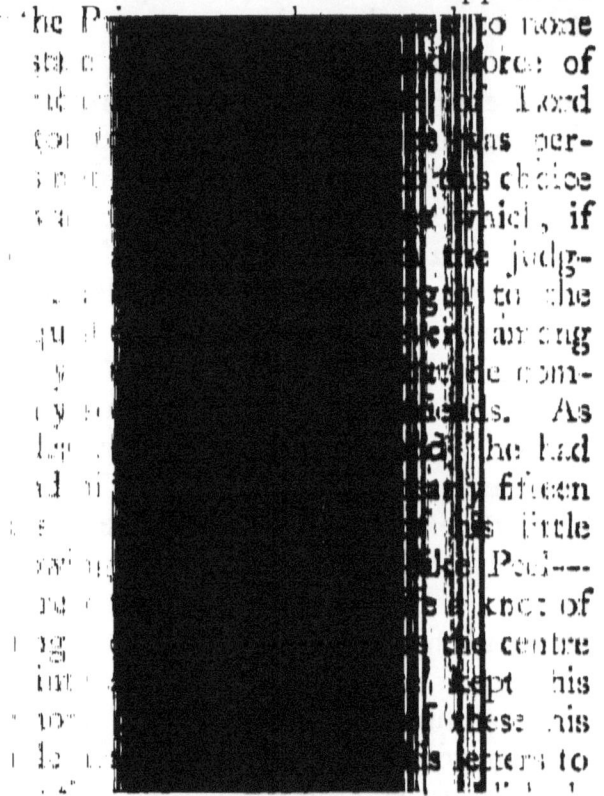

in superlatives, both in writing and in talk, and they were no exaggeration of the depth of his feeling for those he really liked. His profound and admiring regard for women, and his warm affection for his friends, are the salient points in the domestic character of Lord Beaconsfield. That the Queen should, with her sensitive appreciation of these qualities, have come under the charm of her minister's personality was in no way surprising.

Finally, from his proud loyalty to the Hebrew race he never for a moment swerved. For eighteen centuries that race has been slowly taking possession of the civilised world. Through the martyrdom of individual souls Jewish morality has changed the face of the globe. The conduct of the European peoples—modern civilisation as it is called—is their work; while in art, in music, and in letters they have more than held their own. Power, of an overt and conspicuous kind, has, however, for eighteen centuries been denied to men of their blood. Disraeli broke the spell. In July 1878, in the capital of the greatest military nation of our time, among the heroes and statesmen who had created Imperial Germany, among the representatives of the civilised nations of Europe, congregated there to check Russia in her victorious career, and maintain the equal balance of European authority, the most observed and conspicuous personage was not Bismarck, nor Moltke, nor Andrassy, nor any prince nor emperor of them all, but the slim and still youthful figure that with pale and haggard face and slow step, leaning on the arm of his private secretary, was seen day by day to cross the square from the Kaiserhof to the Congress, the representative of the Queen of Great Britain and Ireland and Empress of India—the figure of Lord Beaconsfield the Jew.

VI

THE QUEEN AND MR. GLADSTONE

"His friends lived in dread of his virtues," were the words with which, after alluding to the splendour of his eloquence, unaffected piety, and blameless life, one of the most brilliant of his contemporaries summed up Mr. Gladstone's character as it appeared to men nearly half-a-century ago.

Mr. Gladstone, the writer says, was celebrated far and wide for a more than common liveliness of conscience, and "his friends lived in dread of his virtues." This sally, true of him in his political youth, does not inaptly describe the Mr. Gladstone familiar to all who have known him, and contains the secret of his extraordinary influence, of his strength and

UNIV. OF
CALIFORNIA

weakness, and of his successes and failures. After his retirement from office rather than sanction a grant of public funds to a Catholic college, and his subsequent speech in favour of that very measure, men mocked and marvelled ; but the key to the riddle was under their hand. Sensitiveness to public criticism there was none. Mr. Gladstone has never regarded the opinion of the world so long as he could justify himself to his own lively conscience. He had held views, and published them, incompatible with a proposal he was now conscious of approving on grounds previously unconsidered. He was, however, a member of the Government, and unlike Lord Althorp, who, every morning he awoke, when in office, wished himself dead, to Mr. Gladstone power and responsibilities were a temptation. Was it certain that he was sincere in his approval of this policy? Was it certain that he was unbiassed by his position in the Government, and his desire to retain it? His lively conscience searched him through, and he answered the question by resigning his office. When he was found, as an independent member, supporting the policy he had quitted the Ministry rather than sanction, men laughed, and ever after his friends lived in dread of his virtues. At the same time, his uncommon liveliness of conscience became an established article of faith with those classes of his countrymen to whom conscience is the voice of God, and they gathered round this young man with a faith in his integrity of character which for two generations has never wavered. "Everybody detests Gladstone," wrote Charles Greville in 1857, to whom everybody meant the small coterie of clubmen and drawing-room politicians among whom he habitually moved. London Society, headed by Lord Palmerston, mistrusted Mr. Gladstone, and feared his character. Palmerston "rarely spoke severely of any one," Lord Shaftesbury recorded in his journal: "Bright and Gladstone are the only two of whom he uses strong language." It is a curious commentary upon the tone of Lord Palmerston's mind and the state of feeling he represented that the two statesmen he excepted from his universal charity should have been supreme among those who have established a claim on the affection of the English-speaking world. If more than thirty years ago Society could conceive of no loftier motive to account for Mr. Gladstone's hostility to the Irish Church Establishment than "greed of office," London Society has remained constant to the ideals and judgments of that time, so that Lady Waterford's view, expressed then, would carry to her correspondent no stronger conviction than it would to-day, when she exclaimed, "I have known Mr. Gladstone all my life, and believe in his particularly tender conscientiousness (Canning always said this), and in his justice and feeling of right. Only trust." It was this demand for "trust" that people accustomed to the parliamentary game, to government based on the corruption of constituencies and parliamentary finesse, found then and have found since so difficult to accord. Yet popular instinct has applied to Mr. Gladstone a very different standard. In early days shrewd observers noted that there never was a man so genuinely admired for his earnestness, his deep popular sympathies, and his unflinching courage, and never a man more deeply hated, both for his good points and for his undeniable defects and failings. These were admitted by those who knew and loved him to be his fierceness, his wrath, his irritability, his want of knowledge of men, and his rashness of speech. They explain how it came to pass that he was "loved much less in the House than out of doors," and why it was that the "heart of all Israel was towards him," beyond and not within the precincts of Westminster and St. James Street. Want of knowledge of men is a defect from which any statesman is bound to suffer much tribulation, and in Mr. Gladstone has never been altogether compensated by his unrivalled knowledge of mankind. The contrast here between him and his great rival was marked, and there seemed an almost curiously providential equalising of forces in "how each was seeing and how each was blind," so that if Lord Beaconsfield "knew not mankind, but keenly knew all men," Mr. Gladstone, if he "knew nought of men, yet knew and loved mankind." If knowledge of men is often little more than a clear perception of their weakness, knowledge of mankind is the capacity to feel and evoke their nobler aspirations. It is this latter power which has given Mr. Gladstone his enormous personal influence over the sober-minded and sincerely religious masses of his countrymen, and which would have prompted them to applaud the late Dean of St. Paul's, who, when some clergyman happened to assert in his presence that Mr. Gladstone was a thoroughly insincere man, rose from his chair, pale with emotion, exclaiming, evidently with the strongest suppression of personal feeling, "Insincere! Sir, I tell you that to my knowledge Mr. Gladstone goes from communion with God to the great affairs of State."

It is difficult to realise, at this period of the Queen's long reign, that Mr. Gladstone alone among living servants of the Crown can carry memory and experience back before the days of her accession. Of the relatives and courtiers grouped about the throne in 1837 all have passed away; of the Privy Councillors before whom she took the Oath of her high office not one remains. He is the one living man whose political experience stretches beyond that of the Queen. His is the one figure that for a longer period than that of the Queen has filled the political stage. Sixty-three years have passed since King William, writing to the Leader of the House of Commons, rejoiced "that a young member has come forward in so promising a manner, as Viscount Althorp states Mr. W. E. Gladstone to have done." The Queen was then a child of fourteen, but already, in the not unfriendly eyes of a political opponent, the figure of Mr. Gladstone loomed sufficiently large to form a topic of correspondence between the King and his Chancellor of the Exchequer, while during the whole of the intervening period, for two generations, that figure has loomed larger in the eyes of his countrymen, until his personality at last bade fair to destroy the balance of political life. No one, with the exception of George the Third, has ever been for so long a period reckoned a political force in England. Of precedents in government and of experience in administration, the Queen and Mr. Gladstone alone hold the living record. His retirement has left her supreme in these respects. To her authority and recollection no Minister is able now effectually to oppose the weight of his own; and although she may receive their constitutionally-tendered advice, the Queen must inevitably in future assume towards her Ministers an attitude not unlike that which a mother assumes towards her children.

In all the manifold changes of her reign Mr. Gladstone has borne a part, and not a few he has himself assisted to promote. Alone, among conspicuous Englishmen, he can accompany the Queen back to days when her subjects wore beaver hats and travelled in post-chaises, when Australia was as bleak as Mashonaland, and the Indian Empire a Chartered Company. Should the suspicion, not altogether groundless, that Mr. Gladstone's desire has been to restrict Imperial growth, and to limit the responsibilities of Englishmen to these islands, ever have penetrated the mind of the Queen, she cannot avoid remembering that for over sixty years he has served the Crown, that he has held high office longer than any statesman of her reign, and that within the margin of his career Great Britain has more than doubled in extent, population, and wealth.

When the Queen stepped from her schoolroom at Kensington to the throne, Mr. Gladstone was not only a tried politician but had already served the Crown as a Minister. He had witnessed the last use of a monarch's prerogative to dismiss and replace Ministers. By that act he himself had profited, and had been initiated into the mysteries of office. By the side of this girl Sovereign he must have felt old and experienced. It seemed to him years since he had walked from the Christopher at Eton to the corner of Keat's Lane, with the hand of Canning resting on his shoulder; for Mr. Canning had been Prime Minister since that time, and for ten years had lain in Westminster Abbey. Arthur Hallam, his friend and Eton messmate, was dead too, and already boyhood seemed far behind. While the Queen was learning the alphabet of statecraft under the kindly tutelage of Lord Melbourne, the young man who was to be for many years her Minister had been already remarked by Bunsen as "the first man in England in intellectual power," had attracted the notice of Carlyle as "a certain Mr. Gladstone, an Oxford prize scholar, Tory M.P., and devout Churchman of great talent and hope," and had been described by Macaulay in words which are familiar to every schoolboy. While the mind of the Queen was broadening under the influence and liberal teaching of Peel and Prince Albert, Mr. Gladstone was rapidly shelling off the Tory husk, with which he had found himself by birth and education encased. Already he had begun to discover that he was moving fast away from the associates of his first youth. His critics noticed that he was allied with men who felt differently, thought differently, and spoke differently from him on questions of the highest moment, and proffered the well-worn explanation that he continued to act with them in order to retain office. "His public life" appeared to Lord Shaftesbury, who was opposed to him on many high questions of politics and dogma, "a prolonged effort to retain his principles and yet not lose his position." The truth was, however, that Mr. Gladstone was coming to see that every sound politician and conscientious thinker must sooner or later subject himself to the imputation of inconsistency; that a statesmanlike mind, as Lowell once said, is like a navigable river, making noble bends of concession, seeking ever the broad levels of opinion, and that "the foolish and the dead alone never change their opinion." The young man, who lived in the Albany, and used to ride in the Row on a gray mare, with a "hat, narrow brimmed, high up in the centre of his head, sustained by a crop of thick curly hair," in appearance, according to Lord Malmesbury, not unlike a Roman ecclesiastic, the public advocate of transcendental Erastianism in a militant form, had much to learn and unlearn. "That young man will ruin his fine political career if he persists in writing trash like this," Sir Robert Peel had observed when glancing through Mr. Gladstone's book on *Church and State*; and it was from Sir Robert Peel that Mr. Gladstone, teachable and progressive, then as since, acquired the prescience of Prince Bismarck's maxim that a statesman should serve his country as circumstances require, and not as his own opinions, which are often prejudices, dictate.

Mr. Gladstone's long political career may be roughly divided into two nearly equal portions. It was said of Canning that he was a statesman of conservative opinions and liberal sympathies; and when Bishop Wilberforce, reversing the epigram, wrote of Mr. Gladstone that his sympathies were with the Conservatives and his opinions with the Liberals, it certainly would seem, as the two halves of his life fall into historical perspective, that for the first thirty years and odd, his opinions were constantly struggling to obtain the mastery of his sympathies, whereas in the latter half his sympathies were allowed their proper function of tempering his opinions. The well-remembered opening phrase of his speech at Manchester, after Oxford had discarded him, "At last I am come among you, and am come among you unmuzzled," seems to mark the point at which Mr. Gladstone ceased to be a Peelite, and attained his completeness as the leader of the Liberal party. At the moment, so severe was the wrench from old associations, his career seemed to him to lie behind rather than before him. He had "followed to the grave almost all the friends abreast of whom he had started from the University," and when he laid stress on the fact that "it was hard to find in our whole history a single man who had been permitted to reach the fortieth year of a course of labour similar to his own within the walls of the House of Commons," he little foresaw that he had still before him thirty years of arduous polemics, the most fruitful and the most distinguished years of his long political life.

It was as a trusted lieutenant of Sir Robert Peel that Mr. Gladstone had first come in contact with the Queen, and he cannot have failed in the early days of her married life to have attracted the attention of both herself and Prince Albert. Half-a-century ago Mr. Gladstone was at Windsor Castle on a visit, and "all the ladies were quarrelling for who would have him as a neighbour," while the lady who noted the fact was "envied when it fell to my lot, by the Queen's kind order." That Prince Albert should have been attracted by Mr. Gladstone's earnest and comprehensive mind was natural, for there was much in common between the two men. "It would be difficult to find," Mr. Gladstone said of the Prince, "anywhere a model of life more highly organised, more thoroughly and compactly ordered." If any such life could be found, it would not improbably be Mr. Gladstone's own, of which not many hours, or even half-hours, have been wasted or lost. Omnivorous earnestness in what to others appeared trivialities was a characteristic they possessed in common.

"There seemed to be no branch of human knowledge, no subject of human interest, on which he did not lay his hand; his life was in truth one sustained and perpetual effort to realise the great law of duty to God, and to discharge the heavy debt which he seemed to feel was laid upon him by his high station," are words which, if they describe the Prince, recall quite as vividly their author. And again, when Mr. Gladstone refers to the "secret reconciling of the discharge of incessant and wearing public duty with the cultivation of the inner and domestic life," and declares that "among happy marriages this marriage was exceptional, so nearly did the union of thought, heart, and action both fulfil the ideal, and bring duality near to the borders of identity," it is difficult to think that in thus describing the married life of the Queen, he was not prompted in his use of language by thoughts of his own.

In appreciation of music and art, in love of literature, in "energetic tendency towards social improvement in every form," there was common ground between Mr. Gladstone and the Prince; but there were causes of difference too, and after the death of Sir Robert Peel they assumed larger proportions. Both deeply religious, no two minds could have been theologically further apart. As his intimate friends, the late Cardinal Manning and Mr. Hope Scott, passed over to the Roman faith, a breath of suspicion clung about Mr. Gladstone. Then came the Crimean winter, and the flounderings and fall of Lord Aberdeen's Government. No one knew what course the Peelites would pursue; and uncertainty of political action is anathema in the eyes of constitutional monarchy. Mr. Gladstone, acknowledged to be the ablest man in Parliament, was a "dark horse" in the view of his contemporaries. No one felt sure, after he quitted Lord Palmerston's Government in 1855, where he would find refuge; whether with Mr. Disraeli and Lord Derby, or in the bosom of the Church of Rome. That for some years the Queen had been prejudiced strongly against him was known, but the prejudice had yielded before the pressure exerted by the common friendship of Lord Aberdeen. He, at any rate, appreciated the qualities of his Chancellor of the Exchequer. That Mr. Gladstone would rise to the first place he did not doubt, though it might be gradually and after an interval, when he had turned the hatred of many into affection. "He will turn it if he has the opportunity given him; but he must get over his obstinacy, for he is too honest, if a man can be too honest; and he must attend more to what men think, and as his brother said of him, he must learn to look out of the window." Still he was even then, and it is forty years ago, supreme in the House of Commons; and Lord Aberdeen added, with the right that his intimacy with the Court gave him to speak—"The Queen has quite got over her feeling against him, and likes him much." It is easy to understand that a constitutional Sovereign who, from a position removed from partisanship, surveys the struggle for power between conflicting factions, sees the good and the bad of both sides, minimising the points of difference in principle between them, should be inclined to side with the Minister whose daily effort to act for the best is vividly brought home to her, rather than with the critic whose opposition appears too constant to be sincere. Mr. Gladstone had tried many a fall with Lord Palmerston, and their points of difference were vividly present to the mind of the Queen. It seemed to her that Mr. Gladstone, opposed as he was to the Palmerstonian "civis Romanus sum," or as it has in later years been vulgarly called, a "Jingo" policy, raising objections, as he did, to panic, expenditure on fortifications and armaments, was in reality opposed to the expansion of England within her proper sphere, and hesitated to secure to her the full advantages of her maritime position. He may have been then, as since, too eager a critic, too grasping a custodian of the public funds. Whether this was the case or not, Lord Palmerston fanned the flame :—

Viscount Palmerston hopes to be able to overcome his objections; but, if that should prove impossible, however great the loss to the Government by the retirement of Mr. Gladstone, it would be better to lose Mr. Gladstone than to run the risk of losing Portsmouth and Plymouth.

And again—

Mr. Gladstone told Viscount Palmerston this evening that he wished it to be understood that though acquiescing in the step now taken about the fortifications, he kept himself free to take such course as he may think fit upon that subject next year; to which Viscount Palmerston entirely assented. That course will probably be the same which Mr. Gladstone has taken this year—namely, ineffectual opposition and ultimate acquiescence.

Although Lord Palmerston never stood in the estimation of the Queen in the place of Peel, he was nevertheless Prime Minister, and his words carried weight, and his satire told.

For ten years Mr. Gladstone's position was curious and unique. He was called, in spite of Lord Palmerston's presence and popularity, the first man in Parliament, although he was not the leader of the House. He was acknowledged to be supreme in debate, and to be the highest authority on finance. He was hated by the aristocracy on account of his democratic budgets. He was mistrusted by many because of his High Church sympathies, and even "his friends lived in dread of his virtues." In the eyes of the Sovereign he represented a turbulent and critical element within the

Ministry itself, a Ministry upon which the Queen, together with the large majority of her people, relied as the only administration likely to be safe and durable.

He was, in short, an *enfant terrible* in the world of politics, and as it became clear to every one that a time was rapidly approaching when he must become the Leader of the House of Commons, if not of the Government, no one, from the Queen to the Tadpoles and Tapers of the Liberal Party, looked forward to that time without a feeling of dismay.

With the Oxford election and the death of Lord Palmerston in 1865, the first half of Mr. Gladstone's political career closed, and henceforward he took his place at the head of the Liberal party unfettered, and, as he himself expressed it, unmuzzled. Driven from Oxford—Oxford that he had "loved with a deep and passionate love"—he felt himself free; and from that moment his supremacy over the Party, to which at last, after many years of doubt and hesitation, he finally belonged, was unquestioned. When "old Palmerston was seen to be breaking," it was almost universally believed that his successor would be Mr. Gladstone, although some doubts and fears prevailed that, "having gone a certain way with the Radicals, he would on some Church measure wheel round and break wholly with them."

The Queen had been slowly recovering from the great catastrophe of her life. The Palmerstonian rule, accepted by Parliament and the country as a sort of pax Victoriana, had been of much service to the Queen. Lord Palmerston's great age and long experience soothed the first years of bitter loss. The distrust—to use a mild word—felt by Lord Palmerston for his Chancellor of the Exchequer could not fail to bias the mind of the Queen. That office was one which brought the holder of it into slight contact with the Sovereign, so that the opportunity vouchsafed to Mr. Gladstone of counteracting by personal influence the hostility of the Prime Minister was small. It cannot, therefore, be a matter of surprise that when the long truce came to an end, in view of the pent-up democratic flood at home and lowering clouds abroad, the Queen should have turned, not to Mr. Gladstone, but "to no other than Lord Russell, an old and tried friend of hers, to undertake the arduous duties of Prime Minister, and to carry on the Government."

Mr. Gladstone had anticipated the Queen's decision, and had taken the unusual step of writing to Lord Russell, offering, though sore with conflict, to continue to serve in the capacity of Chancellor of the Exchequer. It was a kindly and thoughtful offer, smoothing the way for an administration, which he felt could not be wholly a continuation, but inevitably a fresh commencement. The centre of gravity in the new Government was misplaced, and it was without the elements of stability. The Prime Minister was a peer, old and frail, while the Leader of the House of Commons was, in the words of the Prime Minister himself, "in eloquence equal to Canning, and in integrity fit to be compared with Lord Althorp." In power of developing the most abstruse proposition, and embracing at once, in his large capacity, the most logical demonstrations, with the most captivating and dazzling rhetoric, Lord Russell's lieutenant had never possessed a superior. If the elder statesman could not then refuse the appeal, pathetic and tempting, once more to take the first place among the Queen's advisers, he knew well that the day was only postponed for a short time when the younger, already the first man in Parliament, would become the First Minister of the Crown.

I felt, said Lord Russell, when the time came, that boldness, which, according to Lord Bacon, is the first quality of a statesman, was required as the primary quality for dealing with the Irish Church, and that no man could dispute the pre-eminence in that quality of Mr. Gladstone.

Even so faithful a friend as Bishop Wilberforce believed that Mr. Gladstone had been "drawn into" his attack on the Irish Church by personal hatred of Mr. Disraeli, and desire to eject him from office; yet it should have been obvious to him, at any rate, that Mr. Gladstone's conversion to the whole body of Liberal opinion was no arbitrary act, but, as he himself described it, the "slow and resistless force" of growing conviction. The process had certainly been slow. It was fourteen years from the death of Peel before Mr. Gladstone finally threw in his lot with the party he was destined to lead in triumph and storm for a generation. It is on this very question of the Irish Church that the relation between the Queen and Mr. Gladstone can best be exemplified; an object-lesson in constitutional government to her successors, and to those rulers who preside over constitutions modelled upon ours. Of her own feeling in regard to the Irish Church we have a record in the words of the Queen herself. Bishop Wilberforce had accompanied Mr. Gladstone to Windsor, when he went to kiss hands on his appointment as Prime Minister.

"Mr. Gladstone is a friend of yours," the Queen said to him in colloquial phrase. "I am sorry he has started this about the Irish Church." The great policy on behalf of which her Prime Minister had fought the General Election, and to carry out which he had been given a majority in Parliament by the people, was clearly not a policy which commended itself to the Queen, who—although the most constitutional Sovereign this country has ever known, liberal in sympathy, and loyal to her Ministers, whatever their party—has claimed for herself, and cannot be denied, the human right of private judgment, and has never forgotten that she is the granddaughter of George the Third. Mr. Gladstone, however, fared better than Mr. Pitt. On 1st March 1869 he introduced the first of his great Irish measures to the House of Commons. Already in the early part of February the Queen had been made acquainted with the lines of the Bill. She was aware of the strong and hostile feeling of the English prelates and of the Conservative party in the House of Lords. The Primacy had recently passed under the auspices of Mr. Disraeli into the hands of a statesman endowed with prudence and courage almost as high as those of Mr. Gladstone himself. To Archbishop Tait the Queen appealed in a letter full of care for the lofty interests she had sworn by her coronation oath to guard.

OSBORNE, 15*th February* 1869.

"The Queen must write a few lines to the Archbishop of Canterbury on the subject of the Irish Church, which makes her very anxious.

. . . The Queen has seen Mr. Gladstone, who shows the most conciliatory disposition. He seems to be really moderate in his views, and anxious, so far as he can properly and consistently do so, to meet the objections of those who would maintain the Irish Church. He at once assured the Queen of his readiness —indeed, his anxiety—to meet the Archbishop and to communicate freely with him on the subject of this important question, and the Queen must express her earnest hope that the Archbishop will meet him in the same spirit. The Government can do nothing that would tend to raise a suspicion of their sincerity in proposing to disestablish the Irish Church, and to withdraw all State endowments from all religious communions in Ireland; but, were these conditions accepted, all other matters connected with the question might, the Queen thinks, become the subject of discussion and negotiation. The Archbishop had best now communicate with Mr. Gladstone direct as to when he can see him.

To the Archbishop the request to act as mediator was not unwelcome.

He immediately sought an interview with Mr. Gladstone. The Prime Minister explained that he had not felt warranted in approaching the Primate or others of whom he knew nothing, except the adverse opinions declared and acted upon by them in the preceding summer. This lack on his part the Queen had kindly undertaken to remove, and he would call at Lambeth Palace on the morrow. It was a memorable interview between two men, either of whom was well qualified by natural aptitudes and congenial tastes to stand in the place of the other. It led ultimately to the passing of the Irish Church Bill through both Houses of Parliament; although the Queen had yet once again to appeal to the Archbishop for assistance, before the House of Lords yielded an assent to the measure. General Grey wrote by the Queen's command.

Mr. Gladstone is not ignorant (indeed the Queen has never concealed her feelings on the subject) how deeply H.M. deplores the necessity under which he conceived himself to lie of raising the question as he has done, or of the apprehensions, of which she cannot divest herself, as to the possible consequences of the measure which he has introduced.

These apprehensions, H.M. is bound to say, still exist in full force. But considering the circumstances under which the measure has come to the House of Lords, the Queen cannot regard, without the greatest alarm, the probable effect of its absolute rejection in that House.

The Archbishop's task was far from easy. He appealed to Mr. Disraeli, and in the Queen's name expressed a strong hope that the Bill might be read a second time in the House of Lords. Successful at this stage, an embittered controversy over the Lords' amendments threatened to wreck the measure. Once more the Queen intervened.

WINDSOR CASTLE, 11*th July* 1869.

The Queen thanks the Archbishop very much for his letter. She is very sensible of the prudence and at the same time the anxiety for the welfare of the Irish Establishment which the Archbishop has manifested in his conduct throughout the debates, and she will be very glad if the amendments which have been adopted at his suggestion lead to the settlement of the question; but to effect this, concessions, the Queen believes, will still have to be made on *both* sides. The Queen must say that she cannot view without alarm the possible consequences of another year of agitation on the Irish Church, and she would ask the Archbishop seriously to consider, in case the concessions to which the Government may agree should not go so far as he may himself wish, whether the postponement of the settlement for another year would not be likely to result in worse rather than in better terms for the Church. The Queen trusts, therefore, that the Archbishop will himself consider, and, as far as he can, endeavour to induce others to consider, any concessions that may be offered by the House of Commons, in the most conciliatory spirit. . . .

The compromise was, however, finally settled, and when the Bill passed, the Primate records with gratitude in his Journal the "great blessing" which the Queen's interest in the welfare of her people ever confers upon the nation; for whatever has been done to secure a fair compromise between conflicting interests, and to avoid a great parliamentary crisis, "thanks to the Queen" are due. The episode depicts in striking colours the bright function of a constitutional

Sovereign. The right of private opinion neither denied nor concealed; perfect loyalty to a Minister whose policy is uncongenial; no attempt at intrigue with the Opposition in Parliament; but an open and successful mediation between the Minister and his opponents, smoothing the path of a great measure of popular change, which, although disliked by her, was approved by the majority of the nation. No object-lesson in democratic monarchy could be more conclusive than this, nor a stronger proof given of prudence in a Monarch and of self-control in a Minister.

It is typical too of the relation for many years between the Queen and the first of her subjects in power and authority. The instance could be varied, but the lesson would read in much the same terms. A Greville might in these later years have heard much with which to fill a gossip's record of the chit-chat of the lobby and the Palace. There were moments of storm in Mr. Gladstone's life, when the popular favour seemed as little secured to him as the smiles of the Court. Driven from the

University he loved, rejected in Lancashire, humiliated at Greenwich, it required all the manly courage and facial pluck of the best type of Englishman to face on a wild autumn afternoon over 20,000 disaffected constituents on Blackheath, and to beat down by force of earnest eloquence their murmurs and threats; it required also the dignity of character and tradition inherited from a long line of predecessors in office silently to accept the rebuke, possibly not unmerited, conveyed by the Queen to her Minister in the letter published by Miss Gordon at the commencement of her brother's correspondence. If the Queen was reluctant in 1880 to accept as her First Minister the statesman who had been designated, only a few months before, by earnest Liberals as a "comet got loose and dashing about the political firmament," it must be remembered that six years earlier that same statesman, grown old in the service of the people, had been ignominiously driven by them from power. If the Queen ever said in a moment of wrath, "I am no longer Queen; Mr. Gladstone is King," it must not be forgotten that the people for whose sake he had given up the peace of his days broke his windows in Harley Street. If in that hour of upheaval in 1886, the Queen wept at parting from her Tory Ministers, and shrank from the meeting with Mr. Gladstone, she only reflected the feelings of those who a few months afterwards hurled him, as he himself expressed it, with contumely from office.

Loyalty within the lines of the constitution is required from a Sovereign; but even a Queen may be permitted to hold if not to express opinions, and to feel if not to show preferences.

Human nature is weak at times, in Monarchs as well as in Democracies, and if the Queen ultimately parted without poignant regret from the Minister who had served the Crown more effectually than any other statesman of the century, it may be remembered with what a sigh of contentment and relief on the retirement of Mr. Pitt George the Third threw himself into the arms of Addington.

The personal service rendered by Mr. Gladstone to the Crown has been gratefully credited to him by his opponents as a redeeming virtue, and admitted laughingly as an amiable vice by his friends. Never by word in public or in private has he been known to reflect on the Throne or on the Sovereign. Brought up under the "shadow of the great name" of Canning, he remembered the example of that statesman. Possibly he recalls how on a summer's day nearly seventy years ago Canning rode down to Eton from the Cottage in Windsor Park, where he was staying with the King, found his son Carlo "staying out" and gossiping with Hallam and Gladstone—three notable figures—over a division in "Pop" in which the *Morning Chronicle* had been retained for that assembly, "in spite of reporting Prize Fights," by the casting vote of Gladstone, and had told the boys that he "could not stay for Ascot races, as he did not think it right that a subject should be cheered in the presence of his Sovereign."

The lesson and the queer punctilio of it may have made an indelible impression, for although ardent in competing for popular favour against political rivals,

Mr. Gladstone has never attempted to overshadow the popularity of the Crown.

Acting with Peel, by timely concession in the great Corn Law quarrel, Mr. Gladstone saved the Throne from the conflicts, possibly from the disasters, of the year 1848. When in recent years of stress and trouble, a word from him would have rallied all the forces of his party against unpopular grants to the Queen's children and relatives, Mr. Gladstone has been found placing his most fervid and impassioned eloquence at the service of the Crown. His feeling towards the Monarchy is described by himself in a letter which reads with peculiar sadness now, written to Prince Albert Victor on attaining his majority in January 1885.

There lies before your Royal Highness in prospect the occupation, I trust at a distant date, of a throne which, to me at least, appears the most illustrious in the world, from its history and associations, from its legal basis, from the weight of the cares it brings, from the loyal love of the people, and from the unparalleled opportunities it gives, in so many ways and in so many regions, of doing good to the almost countless numbers whom the Almighty has placed beneath the sceptre of England.

Not the most loud-mouthed Imperialism could express in more trenchant and telling words respect for the throne of Elizabeth and the England of Mr. Pitt. As a man but one judgment can be formed by posterity of Mr. Gladstone; as a Minister there may be many. Like Mr. Pitt he was a peace Minister, and war was to both men a cause of disaster and failure. Like Mr. Pitt he conceived a great and noble policy for Ireland; and while Mr. Pitt allowed his complete scheme to be wrecked by the scruples of the crowned King of England, Mr. Gladstone permitted his to be maimed by the frailty of the uncrowned King of Ireland.

Neither concession appears to have been necessary, but it must have required all Mr. Gladstone's Homeric lore and reverence to enable him to bear up against the ill-luck of his failure and the disappointment of his hopes. Pluck, however, is a quality which has never failed him. On the 4th December 1890, in the middle of the crisis that was destined to wreck his great policy, he was seen sitting quietly in the Library of the House of Commons reading the *Bride of Lammermoor*. To some this might seem the calm of indifference, but not to those who heard the deep pathos with which he said, "For the past five years I have rolled this stone patiently uphill, and it has now rolled to the bottom again; and I am eighty-one years old."

In relation to those who have had personal intercourse with him a peculiarity of his must never be forgotten. There is a certain transcendental aloofness about Mr. Gladstone's manner with individual men, which creates an impression, probably well founded, that he regards the matter of speech as of far more importance than the speaker himself. Very few can have watched him closely without arriving at the unflattering conclusion that, within limits, his opinion equalises more or less all men. If he has been considered an indifferent judge of men's capacities; and if patronage—which was not ecclesiastical—he has ignored with the lofty coldness of superior minds, to his friends, at any rate to those who had served him, he was loyal; and he never swerved from selecting for office those whom he knew, in preference to those of whom he was personally ignorant. In 1880, when a strong effort was made to induce him to admit into the Cabinet "new blood" as it was called, his reluctance to part with old colleagues was only in one instance with the greatest difficulty overcome. "The next most serious thing to admitting a man into the Cabinet," he said, "is to leave out a man who has once been a member of that body." He had as little idea of cheapening the office as he had of the claims of younger men, because they happened to make clever speeches, or were written up in the Press.

These traits are possibly the leaven of early associations, and the outcome of his Conservative sympathies, but if—as Lord Randolph Churchill said—Mr. Gladstone is found to be in his prime somewhere about the middle of the next century, he will still without doubt exhibit preferences for old friends rather than for new ones, still lament the laxity of costume in the House of Commons, and denounce Speaker Abercromby for permitting members to dine with him in plain evening dress, and still hold Sir Walter Scott to be the superior of all novelists. Whatever their differences on questions of high policy, Mr. Gladstone's prejudices —if the word describes them—must have met with friendly recognition by the Queen. To the throne of England, the most illustrious throne in the world, as he called it—his Conservative sympathies have clung; and the occupant of that throne would have been false to her own record had she not appreciated the extent of the loss to the Sovereign and to the nation when Mr. Gladstone for the last time left Windsor Castle.

At the final Cabinet at which he presided, after Lord Kimberley and Sir William Harcourt had attempted to express what all present felt, as his colleagues left the room, Mr. Gladstone's last words, "God bless you all," spoken in that strong, deep, well-remembered voice, rang in their ears. That blessing, delivered with all the fervour of a mind accustomed to give to every word a full value, was not, we may believe, limited to the Council he was about to quit, but extended beyond the room in Downing Street, to the poorest of the wretched peasantry in whose interest he had laboured throughout his long public life, as well as to the Sovereign, whose reign he must to the end of time be considered to adorn, by his prolonged and strenuous efforts on behalf of popular happiness, by the unaffected simplicity of his life, by his dazzling and splendid eloquence, and by his unswerving fidelity to conscience and to God.

VII

CONCLUSION

The best history has been said to be like the art of Rembrandt, casting a vivid light on certain selected causes, and leaving all the rest in shadow. To illustrate a principle, to point the moral of a character, these are the really effective aims of the historian. In the most famous of his sermons Cardinal Newman explained that men are guided by type, not by argument; that the majority are swayed not so much by the logic of facts as by the idol of the moment; that men are earnest, economical, and pacific when Mr. Gladstone is the most prominent figure in politics, and frivolous, blatant, and careless when the leader of Parliament chanced to be Lord Palmerston; and finally, that the truth cannot be so effectually propagated by any known means as by personal influence. It is from this point of view that the reign of Queen Victoria, and her relation to her Ministers, become of first-rate importance. An exhaustive examination of the character of the Queen, a minute exposition of the policy of her Ministers, are not essential or even necessary for the purpose of explaining this relation, and drawing from it the inference so valuable to students of British Government. Nor is it important nor desirable to attempt to lift the veil of mystery which to a large extent, even in our prying times, conceals from vulgar eyes the influence of the Sovereign. In a great degree mystery and secrecy are vital to the maintenance of royal authority. A monarchy to be stable should subsist in twilight; and an Emperor of China possesses a stronger hold on the imagination of his subjects than a *bon bourgeois* like Louis Philippe of France. Some instinct of this kind has guided the steps of the Queen throughout her reign; so that, in spite of her simple tastes of sympathy more freely given to the poor than to the mighty, and of the light which by her own published books she has thrown on the domestic life of the Court, she has nevertheless contrived to conceal from the public the nature of the power wielded for so many years over her Ministers, as well as the influence she has exercised over social and political events. The Queen has unconsciously managed by her daily life and by her publications to pique rather than to satisfy curiosity; and this is one of the secrets of the regard for her felt not only by her subjects, but by the peoples of both hemispheres. No living Sovereign exercises over the minds of men and women of diverse races so powerful a sway. Not only her own subjects, but the children of every clime have yielded respect to the character of the Queen. Thus it happens that her reign has established precedents for her successors to which they will have as far as possible to conform. To use a modern phrase, the necessity will be enforced upon them of living up to her example. This will be no easy matter; for the Queen has been singularly true to herself, and her life, regu-

legislative chamber, are the terrestrial ideals of these people ; and the Queen, by her personal example and in her political capacity, has fulfilled them. If from the Reform Bill of 1832 to the retirement of Mr. Gladstone in 1894 the Puritan middle classes have governed England, they have certainly no cause to complain of the sympathetic response of the Sovereign to their views and demands. A high standard of virtue had not been hitherto characteristic of the British Hanoverian Court. George the Third had, it is true, endeared himself to the people by his simple domestic life, but the conduct of the Prince Regent altogether destroyed the use of the Court as an example for the people. The two first Georges flaunted their mistresses as openly as any Stuart, while William the Fourth had fathered and ennobled a tribe of illegitimate children. Although in their vices the Guelphs have never displayed the picturesque gallantry of the Stuarts —a family in which political virtue ever varied in inverse ratio to moral conduct, —England, in spite of cheap satire, owes a large debt to the solid virtues of the

Hanoverian House which has presided over the making of the Empire, and culminated in the reign of Queen Victoria. Hanover, under auspicious Providence, gave England a king who could not speak a word of English, and laid firmly in royal unintelligibility the foundation of popular rule. Walpole governed while George the First reigned, and after Walpole came Pitt, and after the father came the son, and after Mr. Pitt came the Reformed Parliament, and the government of England by the English people.

No man, not even a king, can give to the problems of Statecraft more understanding than he possesses, so that the conduct of this line of monarchs should be judged reasonably; and then, after due consideration, fair minds will accord to them a high place in the service roll of English ruling families. Just as Elizabeth rounded off and set a seal on the fame of that Tudor race under which England became one of the first European powers, so Queen Victoria has rounded off and set a seal on the line under which England has become a world-wide Empire. Just as the character and rule of Elizabeth would have made impossible the rule of Mary of Scotland, so the character and rule of Queen Victoria have set a high standard below which it will be impossible for a monarch to fall without personal disaster. The example of Elizabeth led by clear and well-defined steps to the fatal scene in Whitehall, and Charles the First was both victim and example of the sense of contrast in the eyes of a people prone to idealise. The men who led the great rebellion had been taught in boyhood to venerate the figure of the Tudor Queen under whom England had become a mighty power, whose word could be trusted, and who guarded jealously the Protestant faith. In Charles the First they unwillingly admitted to themselves that the antithesis was to be found of these qualities, a discovery fatal both to his authority and to his rule. In like manner future monarchs will have to beware of the example of Queen Victoria.

Out of the slough of the Regency the Queen and Prince Albert raised the Court of England to the first place among nations. For twenty years the loftiest example of domestic and public virtue was conspicuous on the Throne. Upon society the effect was instantaneous, and the decorous behaviour of the Court led, if not to virtue, at any rate to the concealment of vices which had been previously openly flaunted. Paternity was no longer a matter of speculation. Among men and women of noble birth born during the first thirty years of the century, a considerable proportion were illegitimate or notoriously of doubtful parentage. During the next generation the mysteries of the "alcove" were a well-kept secret, and suspicions—if they existed—never degenerated into common gossip; so that men and women now living in high society between the ages of thirty and sixty are conspicuous by their assumption of legitimacy, and by their freedom from suspicion of ambiguous fatherhood. Of the succeeding generation it is too early to express an opinion. Possibly the study of statistics would not expose any great divergence in the morals of the people at large judged by the test of the bar sinister; but statistics deal with humanity in masses and with the great forces which govern civilised and barbarous mankind, among which the example of a Court occupies a trifling place. So that between the acts and pretences of Britons a wide gulf lies open, and statistics count for very little in the eyes of writers in newspapers, or of speakers at public meetings. Popular opinion stereotyped in mob oratory and the morning papers has decided that the Victorian type is essential to kingship, and under the fiercer light which beats nowadays on every step of the throne, no departure from that type could be undertaken with impunity. It was said of George the Third and his Court that they were not in Society, and the same remark might by cavillers be applied to the Court of Queen Victoria since December 1861; but unlike George the Third, whose late life sank into Shakespearian gloom, the Queen has ever conspicuously maintained her high moral attitude of benevolence, of personal sympathy in sorrow, of tender gratitude for public service, of tender regard for misfortune, pain, or death in the meanest of her subjects. To the English-speaking peoples all over the world she has stood in the relation of a mother to her children. Queen Elizabeth, even in old age, to use the suggestive language of romance, was the mistress of every one of her subjects; Queen Victoria has been and is the veritable mother of her people.

If in the domain of moral conduct a notable example has been set by the Queen, her constitutional behaviour has established a series of precedents which cannot fail to guide her successors. These resolve themselves naturally under two heads, into her exercise of the royal prerogative, and into her personal relation to her Ministers.

It is a common mistake to assume that because the prerogatives of the Crown have apparently lain dormant for over half-a-century, they have ceased to be reckoned a factor of the constitution. No experienced Minister would be guilty of ignoring this silent force imperceptibly swaying the tides of political life. The Queen has never once during her long reign exercised her prerogative in a coercive or revolutionary spirit. She has never dissolved Parliament except in accordance with the advice of her Ministers, or dismissed from her counsels advisers who commanded a majority in the House of Commons.

The dismissal of the Whig Government in 1834 by William the Fourth, an act futile of consequences, has not been imitated by the Queen; nor has she, like her uncle, threatened to overcome the resistance of one branch of the legislature and to redress the balance of parties by the creation of Peers. On all occasions when parties have clashed, or the Houses of Parliament have differed, the present Sovereign has been content to exercise the influence of reason in the direction of compromise, and where this was impossible, has left the arbitration to the electorate.

It is impossible at the present time, with however light a hand, to touch upon the relation of the Queen to the present Prime Minister, Lord Salisbury, or to discuss the short period of Lord Rosebery's rule. That the influence of the Sovereign upon her Ministers has diminished, neither of them would probably assert, nor has the loyalty with which the support of the Crown was accorded to them in turn been in any degree lessened from that which supported Peel through the troublous Corn Law days.

Queen Victoria's rule has extended over a longer period, day for day, than that of any British Sovereign; and during the whole of that long reign she has exhibited to her people qualities hitherto unassociated with the name of King or Queen—qualities of heart which have endeared her not only to her own people, but to millions to whom her name stands for every womanly virtue, and qualities of mind which not only have enabled her to guide and sustain a long series of the ablest Englishmen engaged in the task of ruling, but have set such a mark upon the history of her country, that constitutional Monarchy must be for ever associated with her reign, and mainly founded upon her example.

Printed by R. & R. CLARK, LIMITED, *Edinburgh.*

www.ingramcontent.com/pod-product-compliance
Lightning Source LLC
Chambersburg PA
CBHW030117030726
47498CB00007B/2434
* 9 7 8 3 3 3 7 1 6 8 2 1 6 *